Wrong Acquaintance

A novel by T.C. Beatty

Order this book online at www.trafford.com
or email orders@trafford.com

Most Trafford titles are also available at major online book retailers.

Printed in Victoria, BC, Canada.

ISBN: 978-1-4269-2242-8 (soft)
ISBN: 978-1-4269-2243-5 (hard)

Library of Congress Control Number: 2009940715

*Our mission is to efficiently provide the world's finest, most comprehensive book publishing
service, enabling every author to experience success. To find out how to publish your
book, your way, and have it available worldwide, visit us online at www.trafford.com*

Trafford rev. 1/19/2010

 www.trafford.com

North America & international
toll-free: 1 888 232 4444 (USA & Canada)
phone: 250 383 6864 ♦ fax: 812 355 4082

To Mark Penn...

Chapter 1

"Ma," Billy Joe expressed in embarrassment. "Not the little league pictures. I didn't have my two front teeth."

"Billy, that doesn't matter. You still had a million dollar smile, even with no teeth," Mrs. Jackson replied, hugging her son.

"I'll just be happy when this is all over. I just keep having to go to the bathroom. I ain't ever had to pee this often. Every few minutes too," Joe bluntly stated.

"Maybe you got a STD, a sexually transmitted disease," his sister joked.

"A STD?"

"Sex- ually transmitted. You are starting to show signs."

"I don't itch, and why don't you mind your own business."

"Well, in health class, we talked about it. You can get 'em," Chrissy warned.

"Well, I am not active right now to get 'em," Billy tells Chrissy while slamming the bathroom door.

The local television stations had been calling the Jackson's residence to get an interview after the draft. Billy Joe and his family agreed to do the interview in their home.

Hundreds of miles away in New York were several draft potentials. Dressed in their finest suits, the young men looked like they were not going from rags to riches, but from riches to more riches. The players who flew in for the draft looked confident, yet nervous. It was a Saturday afternoon in New York. The excitement had been built up for months. Who would go first round? Today, many dreams would come true. It was the NFL draft day. The Saint Louis Rams had first pick. Overall, the NFL was looking for fresh tight ends and running backs, hopefully with the athletic build and abilities of retired, running back, Eddie George.

"Let's pray, baby," the older lady said.

"Ok, mamma. You are going to lead?"

"No, baby, I want you to lead it before the commissioner starts."

Mother and son bowed their heads in prayer. "Dear heavenly father, thank you for this day. Thank you for bringing me this far. I thank you for my mother, allowing her to sacrifice so much. She went without so I could have. She has worked so hard to be the best momma in the world, even when daddy left us. I want to be able to return the wonderful deeds. Grant me those opportunities. In thee, we pray, Amen."

Momma Annie was fighting back tears after hearing her only son's prayer. "Baby, I didn't know you felt like that," expressed Mrs. Patterson, looking into her son, Andre's eyes. "Yes, Momma. You deserve the best. I'm going to take care of you the way I've always wanted to since daddy left us. Momma, I love you." Annie tearfully replied, "Baby, I love you too."

The draft began after the commissioner had called for everyone's attention. All NFL teams were listed. "1st round-St. Louis Rams: Mark Sneider, Running Back, Ohio State University; New Orleans Saints: Zac Langly, Outside linebacker, University of Texas; New York Jets: Morreo Peavely, Quarterback, Northwestern University." The crowd roared with excitement as ESPN viewers watched with admiration. "Nashville Sphinx: Billy Joe Jackson, Quarterback, Texas A&M; Chicago Bears: Timothy Stallings, Linebacker, UCLA. The commissioner continued with the second round picks as Andre clinched his mother's hand tighter. "Washington Redskins, Jonathon Stover, Tight-end, Florida State University; Nashville Sphinx: Andre Patterson, Wide Receiver, University of Illinois."

"Yes!" Andre released his tension as he jumped for joy with his mother. He was not concerned he went second round even though his agent and the media predicted he would be a first round draft pick. Andre subdued his boisterous, charismatic nature in order for the commissioner to finish. When Mark Flintman finished, the reporters rushed to get an interview with Andre, asking about his new home in Nashville.

"Nashville is a great town. In fact, I considered attending Tennessee State University until the Chief at University of Illinois heavily recruited me in state. Nevertheless, I'm new in baby blue. Yes, new in baby blue." Andre charismatically chanted, "I am proud to be a new Nashville Sphinx."

As the media slowly died away to another draft pick, Momma Annie hugged her son, mumbling, "My baby, my baby," with tears of joy falling quickly from her face. Andre picked his mother up like a feather over his shoulder shouting, "Momma, we did it. We did it. Yes, hell yeah, momma, we did it." Annie, being a calm, subdued, yet dynamic woman interjected, "Boy, if you don't put me down, I'm going to bite like Mike Tyson."

"Alright, momma. All right. Let me take you to dinner," he said.

In Cleveland, Texas, the hometown media had begun interviewing Billy Joe Jackson.

"Billy, you do wish the Sphinx had stayed in Houston so you wouldn't have to travel so far?" asked the reporter.

"That would have been nice. Well, we'll just have to make special plans for the whole gang to come see me play every weekend in Nashville," Billy suggested.

"Billy, I take it you are definitely ready to party."

"Well, I tell ya, I'm ready to praise the Lord. The church is throwing me a brunch. They have been so prayerful and supportive of me over the years. They just want me to continue to reap all the goodness the Almighty has in store for me just from following his word. You get what you deserve. If you do good, and follow in God's footsteps, you have nothing to fear. Nothing! God protects his own from evil forces. I'm just thankful he saved me," Billy religiously expressed.

The reporter was standing in awe of the athlete's religious based comments on air. Reacting spontaneously, the reporter thought of what to say live on air to end this interview.

"There, we have it. Billy Joe Jackson, as you can tell is thankful to be picked up by the Tennessee Sphinx. We expect to see dynamic plays out of the Texas A&M graduate. Back to you at the news desk." Removing his microphone, the reporter said to the cameraman, "Good rap."

Chapter 2

Andre returned to Champagne, Illinois to party with his teammates, classmates, hometown boys, fans, and an abundance of women. The party was at Kams Sports Bar. As soon as he unpacked his bags and changed clothes, he went straight to the party scene to meet up with Mark Medrano and Phillip Andrews who had been picked up as free agents by the New York Jets and the San Francisco 49ers, respectively. They were the only three to go to the NFL from the University of Illinois this season.

As Andre entered Kams, everyone hushed and suddenly shouted, "Cheers!" A Budweiser Select was given to him. He chuckled, laughed, and shouted to the packed club, "Who da Man?" As he wavered his way through the smell of beer and dancing people, he spotted teammates, Mark and Phillip. Andre shouted, "Hey Medrano, What's up?" Medrano reached out and gave him a big hug. Phillip laughingly said, "We did it. It's fucking on!" The teammates made a festive toast, nearly spilling half the beer. "To the NFL!!"

People continuously greeted them with congratulations. The intensity of the party never diminished; the smell of beer was everywhere. As Andre took the center floor to get his "dance groove on," he bumped into many of his old classmates from the Business School. They all jokingly celebrated with Andre about going to the Tennessee Sphinx and hoping for free tickets to the Bears vs. Sphinx game. Andre just gave a head nod and laughed.

Suddenly, he felt this heavy pull on his red sports shirt. At first, he thought he was caught onto something as he worked his way through the crowd. When he finally turned to see what was pulling on him, he was surprised to see one of his high school buddies, Arteah.

"Congrats, 'Dre," she yelled with joy. "You did it."

"What are you doing down here?" asked Andre. "I'm sure you have finals to start preparing for."

"Yeah, Yeah. Now, you know I am not one for the drinking scene, but I couldn't resist seeing my hometown buddy's celebration into the N-F-L. I wouldn't miss this for the world. Are you not happy to see me?" Arteah inquired.

Andre smiling, "Yeah, I know that's why I'm surprised as hell. Arteah, it's good seeing you, girl. I haven't seen you since you broke up with Roderick."

"Boy, don't lie like that; you saw me last year when I came down from Illinois State to your homecoming game to see you play." Arteah recalled.

"Oh yeah, that's right," Andrea remembered.

They danced the night away in close quarters with other carefree students. The DJ played some old disco music such as "Car Wash," and a medley of George Clinton P-Funk tunes. They laughed as Arteah recalled a dance they did in junior high school called the "Smurf." Andre, then remembered the "Swoop" with the neck movements and the "PeeWee Herman" dances.

Leaning on one another, they burst into laughter. As the music got funky, the funkier they danced. They naturally moved to the high energetic tunes, quoting lyrics like skilled rappers. As the sweat poured down their backs and foreheads, drenching their shirts, they kept in motion, even when they were beginning to tire. Andre pulled a small white cloth from his back pocket and gripped it in his hand. He lifted the towel to Arteah's forehead and gently wiped away her sweat. Andre, blotting away the sweat on her back and neck, left Arteah starring up at him, wondering what compelled him to sweetly touch her. She felt awkward; yet, she was instantly and sensuously aroused by Andre's touch in front of everyone on the dance floor. The moment left her speechless and confused, yet she appreciated his towel touch. It was so caring.

After he cooled her down a bit, he wiped his own sweat with such satisfaction.

"That felt good, didn't it?" asked Andre.

"Yeah, thanks. That was very considerate," Arteah replied.

"You're welcome, home girl. I'm just happy to see you. Are you ready to break out of here? I've gotta idea. Let's take a walk."

"A walk? Arteah repeated. Where are we going to walk to?"

"Wherever…till we get tired. Let's just walk."

"Alright, but I need to drive my car over to your apartment. I really planned on going back to I-State tonight. I just wanted to come down to personally congratulate you on your success." expressed Arteah.

"Teah, it is too late to be on the highway this time of night," Andre warned.

"Now, you know I can make the drive in 40 minutes. Ain't nothing but a wing," Arteah sarcastically stated. They both replied, "Nothing but a chicken wing."

As they made their way through the crowd to the door, the weather suddenly looked misty, like it would rain or at least sprinkle. Andre walked Arteah to her Volkswagen, then she gave him a lift back to his car around the corner. Andre hopped into his blue Blazer and led the way back to his apartment on Nevada Street.

Andre chose to live to the east of campus, because it was quiet. Most of his teammates lived on the Healey Street, south of Green Street, where there was something always going on. As Arteah got out of her car and into his truck, Andre asked her if she was hungry. She said she only wanted something to drink. So they went to the corner gas station and bought Minute Maid fruit punch drinks. Afterward, Andre drove to the FAR/PAR dorms and parked. They walked across to the park filled with an abundance of trees and sat on one of the benches.

"This park is nice and peaceful," commented Arteah. "Trees are one of the most important, if not the most important living organisms on earth. One day, I'm going to become a revolutionary advocate for rainforest preservations. I just truly believe the cure for HIV will be found with extracts from the rainforest, but if we keep destroying them, by putting up fancy resorts and things, we'll never know. Did you know we get shampoo from plant extracts taken from the rainforest?"

"No, I didn't know that, "Andre replied.

"Furniture oil too and the list goes on and on."

"Yeah, I see you are very serious about rainforest issues," noticed Andre.

"Heck yeah. Most people don't have a clue. We live in a society where most of America is really on a 9th grade level, even though they have high school diplomas. Most Americans know nothing about Geography and the way people live outside their own little domain. It's just sad, and we think we are working towards a multicultural society. That's marketing bullshit to make a dollar. You should know Andre; you're majoring in Business," Arteah intensely remarked.

"I see what you are saying, but life goes on. Get what you can while you can," Andre interjected.

"True. That's true, but if you don't stand for something, you'll fall for anything," said Arteah.

Arteah had views on everything in life. She was very knowledgeable, a very well studied student. Arteah had a fascinating analytical mind that would tick and tick with thoughts and ideologies.

Andre sincerely commented, "Arteah, I've always admired you since junior high school. You always have been 'TEAH. I really dig that, girl. That's good shit. I know you're graduating with an Education-Social Studies degree, right? But what are your dreams? What are your highest aspirations?"

"Dre, you are so damned crazy. If I were born male, 6'4", 230 pounds, I'd be a wide receiver for…let's see…the Nashville Sphinx," she said jokingly.

"Naw, for real. No bulling. I," she hesitatingly looked up at the midnight blue sky "want to develop an economic trading system for African descent people across the world. I want African Americans to have economic ties to South Africa and

9

western Africa. I want African Americans to have economical ties to Haiti, and Brazil. I want us to be connected like the stars in the sky, like the big dipper. It's not meant to abuse economic advantages that we'll gain, but to empower and train our own. To become self-reliant. You know, I get so tired of seeing poverty amongst our people.

"Aren't you blunt and opinionated," Andre interjected.

"What?!"

"TEAH! I hear you. You may very well be the next Harold Washington of Chicago," Andre boisterously said.

Calming her intellectual voice, Arteah asked, "How's your love life or should I say sex life? We both know you have been very loose since junior high."

"Teah, you're a liar. I've never have been very loose," Andre defensively replied. "I just know where to go."

"Alright, lick 'em low lover," she laughingly said.

"But I have been chilled for a while."

"What?" she raised her voice to a higher pitch. "Chilled?! Boy, lightening is about to strike. Let me get as far away as possible. You know God don't like ugly," she grinned.

"Well, I don't want to get 'caught up' before I go into the NFL. Some woman trapping me with a child, and I'll have to pay child support for eighteen years, even though I'll be able to afford it," he smirked.

"See I really need a woman like you, but you know me a little too well. I can't really pull any shit. If I step to you, I'd have to come correct, and I ain't ready to come fully correct. Art, I know I still do have a little 'ho' in me."

"Andre Patterson, are you trying to come on to me? Do I stimulate your mind that much?" asked Arteah.

"Well, actually, it's your sensuous body that keeps in motion in my mind. Girl, the way you were dancing back at Kams almost drove me crazy. You are definitely the sexiest woman I know. God did not make a mistake when he made you. You should be Jet magazine's "Beauty of the Week," not to mention your mind. You have this classy, home girl style that can almost intimidate a man if he ain't got his shit together. I like your high standards; that's definitely how you've kept yourself up. You ain't never having a man stressing you out. You ain't got time for the bullshit. You wanna save the trees and shit."

Arteah smiling, "Dre, you are beyond crazy."

"Art, you are going to go far. You really look like a professor heading up the African American Studies Department at Harvard University, especially with your creative ideologies. I have to admit; you remind me of my mother. She is always speaking, preaching and teaching. You know I really appreciate that in you. One day, I'll settle down. After I get all of my 'spiritec' ways out of my system, I know I can be a good man."

"What in the hell is "spiritec," asked Arteah.

"You know, when your spirit blows you from woman to woman. It's not love. It's like the wind just pushes you, and you don't want to fight the wind. So you just indulge with the new spirit of the day. Then it blows you elsewhere, and you indulge with no regrets. Spiritec! It's a spiritual force, but it's not grounded with any principles. It's total freedom."

Arteah sincerely warned, "I think in time, Andre, you'll learn to find freedom within principles. Eventually, the freedom you're talking about appears to be free, but everything has consequences, even the consequences of so-called "spiritec."

"Look it's really about to rain. Let's walk and look at some for the nice homes," suggested Arteah.

"In the rain," asked Andre.

"Oh, are you scared of the rain now? You're going to cry, because you're about to get your shirt soaked again?"

Arteah simply smirked at Andre.

They started walking. As Andre looked down at Arteah, she shook her head in disbelief.

"I don't believe you've got me walking at 3:30 a.m. in the morning in the rain."

Arteah, stealing an array of tulips along the way to make a treasured bouquet, smelled her yellow and red tulips. Andre leaned closer to Arteah to also smell her flowers.

"Yeah, they smell nice, but I ain't going to jail when these affluent people realize you are the tulip bandit of the night," remarked Andre.

"Shut up, Dre, Arteah whispered, lightly punching him in the arm.

Arteah, attaching her arm to his arm, walked in total surrender to nature. She was not concerned about her fallen curls. She breathed in long breaths, as if she were meditating. For the first time, silence fell upon both of them. Andre had no words, as Arteah had exhausted her intellectual thoughts. It was rather awkward for the two since both were extreme extroverts. Even though no words came forth from their mouths, silence began to speak.

The soft raindrops began to council them both. The rain began to connect them. Andre slid his hand down to embrace Arteah's hand. Firmly cuddling her hand, Andre told her he respected her.

"Art, I think you have one of the most beautiful spirits I've ever seen. It radiates, and that is what makes you beautiful, even though God has given you physical beauty too."

"Thanks. You are so kind and considerate."

"I don't want you to think I'm bullshitting you. I really truly respect you and admire you. Ok, I even think I could madly fall in love with you, event to the point I would not desire any other woman. I would feel your warm hands, even when I'm alone."

"What?" Arteah surprisingly looked in his eyes.

"I just have this vibe you are the woman I need to be with, but I am too scared I'll just screw up. I'll result to my old habits. I do not want to send you through the ringer like my dad did my mom. It's just not fair. I'm too scared to even think about a committed relationship. I'm really a coward when it comes to that issue. I don't know if this is just the nature of a young man or what. All I know is that you deserve someone who can truly come correct. I know I have that type of man in me, but it wants to hide, or maybe he's just too chicken shit to come forward," Andre sincerely expressed.

"Dre, where is all of this coming from?"

"I don't know. Maybe the rain? True confessions."

Arteah added, "I don't know what to say either. I do feel an exciting interaction between us that is scary. We are going in such divergent directions. You are going to Nashville and I'm thinking about relocating to Denver to teach, so I can be near the mountains. I do think you are a neat guy, who is a rainmaker. You always take advantage of all of your opportunities. You have charisma, like Dion Sanders. You are just full of life. You clearly know your weaknesses and strengths, and you never let your weaknesses overtake your strengths, maybe because you are conscious of them. I admire that I could never view you as a liar.

Andrea pulled her nearer to him and gave her a teddy bear styled hug. "Thanks, I'll take that since it's coming from you," replied Andre.

By this time, the two were just passing the President's house.

"You think it's too late to stop by and say hi to the Pres.?" joked Andre.

In passing, they both looked at the mansion with admiration. On the side of the President's home were enormous trees, mostly pine trees. The scent of the pine trees drew them both in that direction.

"You know, I never realized there were all of these trees on the side of the President's home, and I pass this way almost everyday. Seriously, I had never paid any attention to how tall these trees are," Andre commented in discover.

"Yeah, this is beautiful," she said.

The rain had begun to subdue to just sprinkles. The two friends sat down on the grass to rest a bit, since they had danced, then walked and talked the entire night away. She laid her bouquet of tulips on the grass; then, she rested her exhausted head upon his chest, and he comforted her as silence once again began to talk. Arteah was completely relaxed as she felt safe in Andre's arms. She began to doze off to sleep. Her intuition allowed her not to worry. She truly trusted Andre with her safety.

Andre was in deep thought trying to comprehend why this encounter happened now, especially considering he has known Arteah since junior high school. The only thing he knew was that he felt 100% comfortable around her. She understood him completely. After all, Andre thought she was the sexiest, most alluring woman he had ever known. She possessed a mystique that could mesmerize, tantalize and offer insight with delight. As Arteah turned her head to the other side, Andre lifted her chin up. He slowly bent his head to look at her face in enjoyable study.

He touched her eyebrows; then, he followed the shape of her nose with his index finger. Slowly making his way to her mouth, he affectionately covered her mouth with his fingers. His lips touched her delicate ear, even though he wanted to kiss her lips. She awoke to his touch and looked him in the eyes. He felt as if Arteah had opened up an undiscovered side of him that he had never felt before. Andre could actually feel the depths of his emotions, he usually ran through faster than Michael Johnson could run the 200-meter dash. No longer could he contain his emotions, he finally kissed her passionately.

While touching her hair with his strong, gentle hands, he gently unbuttoned her pink, silk shirt, uncovering her sheer, rosy-colored bra. Andre was amazed at how her nipples stood at attention through her sheer bra for him. He massaged her neck as she uplifted, attempting to take her bra off completely. As Arteah returned to her relaxed position in Andre's arms, he said in a whispering tone, "Looka here, don't you ever de-size your breast. They are perfect. Absolutely perfect."

Arteah lay completely on the grass. Andre then touched her nipples with awe, observing their size in the palm of his huge hand. He touched her cup with such sensitivity. With his tongue, he touched underneath her breast, circling around her right nipple, but never licking her nipple. He blew, like a cool breeze, on her perky mountainous nipples immediately. He blew on the right breast, which was jealous for attention. Again, Andre started from the bottom of her left breast and mystically worked his soft, firm tongue around her nipple. In release, Andre passionately kissed her nipple as he rubs his hands through her loosely fallen curled hair. Arteah felt such sensations across her body as the rain began to fall on her forehead.

In the midst of all the kinetic energy, their clothes were removed like the speed of flash lightening. She could smell the scent of the grass and pine trees. Andre, for the first time looked like the sexiest man she had ever seen. His body was atop hers. The rain gently fell on his buttocks. As Arteah stroked her wet index finger from his butt hole to the small of his back and even up to Andre's chiseled neck, Andre moaned with disbelief of contentment. He had never felt this free and expressively uninhibited. They both knew. They both knew they could not have intercourse, because they had not protection. All they could do was titillate.

Neither one of them expected the rain would bring out such compassionate, intimate feelings. Were they already there, or did the scent of the moist grass and trees seduce them both? As Andre kissed Arteah's fingers, she breathlessly expressed, "Andre, you…you…you feel."

"What?" as Andre looked into her eyes.

Trying to contain her words, she replied, "Good…Good!"

"Good, baby?" he mumbled as he caressed her feet with his tongue.

Andre closed his eyes as he intensely sucked each and every one of Arteah's rosy pink toes. While he was tongue massaging one foot, he hand massaged the other. Art's body made love jerks. She needed to hold onto something. As she grabbed for grass on both sides of her, she felt the stem of her stolen tulips.

She pulled the canary yellow and red tulips closer to her. She held the small bouquet over her head as she said "Oh my God!"

Andre began to explore between her thick, shapely toned thighs. Art had legs of a stallion. Andre began to bite the inside of her thighs. As he moved closer up her thighs, working his way up to the lips of her vagina, Arteah broke the stems of the tulips in half. She moaned, "Sweetheart." In a timeless moment, Andre slid up to her face and looked at her. In a completely peaceful voice he expressed, "You are really special to me." He kissed her giving her the fire of his heart. He kissed her intensely like he loved her. She did not know how to read the kiss, but she soulfully submitted to the intensity of his kiss. His fire filled kiss lit her emotions.

"Firefly is what you are," he smilingly interjected. "You are a creature of the night that draws me in with your mystical light."

"Now, I'm a beetle?" Arteah inquired.

"Yeah,…Art…a fiery one that shines when it chooses to shine. I can't believe it's almost sunrise. We'd better get moving before the President takes a morning walk and catches us butt naked on his lawn. What could we possibly say?" briefed Andre.

"I wouldn't say anything," Arteah laughed. "I don't go here, but he knows you. You are one of the finest athletic students to graduate from the University of Illinois, and I do mean literally. You would be more embarrassed than me. In fact, I would not care."

"Yeah, right. You'd care if he charged you with a misdemeanor and then someone leaked it to the press and had your name of the front page of some hilarious Enquirer styled magazine. "I-state/U of I students caught nude by President Roberson."

"President who? President Clinton?" asked Arteah.

Andre replied, "Well, I don't think President Clinton would mind."

As they joked about the adventures of the night while putting their clothes on, the twosome eventually made it back to the FAR dorm area where Andre's car was parked.

After breakfast, Andre walked Arteah to her car. They both had puffy eyes from sleep deprivation. Andre picked Arteah up and hugged her; then, he gazed into her eyes and said, "Thanks for coming. I really appreciate your support and affection, even though you teased the hell out of me." He passionately kissed her one last time, before she got in her car and zoomed back to Illinois State University.

Chapter 3

So much time had escaped since Arteah last saw Andre. After graduation, she accepted a teaching position in a Magnet school on the South Side of Chicago. She was back at home in the neighborhood, attempting to make a difference in young students' lives. Yet, every other weekend, her best friend, Sherika, and her were always planning and taking mini vacations. Arteah wanted to explore the world, to see as much as she could. After all, she spent the last four years studying. She attended every popular festival in the region. Arteah was determined to enjoy single hood. She maintained a healthy dating life. The men that were attracted to her did not mind offering her the world.

In fact, some guys felt they wanted to marry her by the third date. Arteah was often leery of those types. In a sassy voice, she would girl talk with Sherika that she was perfect for their expectations, but they were imperfect for her expectations. She felt she deserved a very, traditional, masculine man, not a feminine man who'd expect her to drive and go Dutch. She would often have to tell men about their role. "You are the man, and I am the woman. You are supposed to be masculine, and I am feminine. If you can't treat me like the lady I am, have a great, feminine life!"

Moreover, dating had taken a toll. Though Arteah enjoyed the capricious outing and often times comedic skits she participated in on dates, she yearned for a committed relationship, one with potential to evolve into a marriage. A few gentlemen asked her for a committed relationship; she refused to avoid losing control and falling in love with someone she knew she would have pet peeves with in the long run, thus eventually driving her crazy. She could not stand a smoker, a weed user, a man who talked too slow, a man who walked too slow, a man who did not a dream, and a man who did not make her feel like a goddess.

"Is that too much to ask for, Sherika?" she asked.

"Girl, I hear you. It's gotten pretty bad. You either find a man who is nice and weak or broke, trifling men who are not taking care of their responsibilities or you find a strong man who is highly degreed, taking care of his career business, yet treats you like a number. To be honest, those are the worst men- educated pimps. They think like…

Why have one woman when I can have 5 to 6 women chasing me. I can afford it. It's sad to think, Art, that what we have to choose between is love and class. Hell, all the good men in church are married. I want a classy man who loves me and not a trashy, trifling man who loves me. Surely, I don't want a wealthy man who treats me like trash. Why do we feel like we have to settle?" ranted Sherika.

"You know what; I think it's America. I hear the men in Paris are nice, gentlemen and really artsy. Sherika, you hear me girl, I'm moving to Paris. I'm leaving America. Why limit myself to Chicagoans or just Americans. Hell, we can choose from Haitians, Jamaicans, South Americans, Europeans, South Africans, and Nigerians," responded Arteah.

Sherika interjected, "I know about Nigerians, I hear they are too possessive, yet they are good providers."

"Plus all of Asia," added Arteah.

"Art, you have lost your mind. I want to marry an African American. Our culture is screwed up enough!"

"I feel you girl. All I'm saying is that I don't think we should limit our potential for happiness. We should not settle for a nice, trifling man. We should go for a nice, handsome, financially stable man, who can fulfill our Cinderella dreams," raved Arteah.

"You are talking Cinderella visions like it's B.C., before Christ," bluntly stated Sherika.

"Sherika, black women don't dream anymore. We don't believe we can conquer the world and have a cherry as a treat. We work too hard to prove ourselves, to whom? Why are we always seeking validation to be super women. Well, sweetie, I ain't a superwoman. I am a goddess, who deserves a god. I live in paradise and America is a small piece of the Paradise and Chicago is the crumb. Now, I love Chicago, but I think I need to explore new horizons. I don't know…maybe I'll take up photography and write shorts stories for the National Geographic. Our perspectives need be represented."

"Ok, Art. Go be artsy. I've always known you were the daredevil. You'll go skydiving and parasailing in a minute. You just live on the edge. I, on the other hand, am the smooth sailor. You would not see me hopping out of airplanes, over mountains nor grasslands. Sometimes, I don't even know why I hang out with a nut like you," jokingly remarked Sherika.

"Because, darling, sweetie pie, you are crazy too; you just haven't come to terms with it. I am crazy and know that I am a little touched by an angel," said Arteah.

They both laughed.

"Let's go get some ice cream. I think German Chocolate is back this season," suggested Arteah.

"Girl, it's getting kind of nippy for ice cream."

In a singing voice, "Sherika, this is the best time to eat it. When it is not that hot, it tastes better anyways. We can walk around to Baskin Robbins."

"Actually I wouldn't mind a malt. Let me go slide on a jacket and put my new boots on," Sherika said.

As they left out of Sherika's apartment to make it down the street around the corner, they talked about life at Illinois State University together. Their close social circle of four was separated. Dana went on to medical school at Xavier, and Lydia went to law school at Michigan. They would occasionally touch base through three-way connections. What they experienced at Illinois State together was forever cherished.

Recently, Sherika had landed a public relations position for the Cubs baseball club. Sherika found her new position exciting, yet challenging. Art enjoyed teaching Social Studies; her class was vivacious. Her students yearned to learn.

They finally made it to Baskin Robbins and ordered. Arteah asked for two scoops of German Chocolate in a cup, and Sherika had the Oreo's Cookies and Cream malt. They sat at one of the tables near the window, so they could see people walk by as they indulged in their frozen treats.

"Sherika, I do love Chicago. It's home. There's nothing like the Taste of Chicago and all the other festivals. I even love the weather, as long as they close school, so I won't have to teach on blizzard days. But I feel I want to live somewhere else, just for a little while, to explore, and to see how other people are living. What do people do for fun in Alaska this time of year? What do people do in Cuba for the holidays? Have those people ever seen snow in their lives? Well, I haven't experienced a hurricane, but we've seen our share of blizzards. So I guess it all balances out. Everybody has something dynamic they must go through in life. I wonder how they cope. They wonder how we cope; yet we cope, if we're strong enough and lucky enough."

"I feel you girl," Sherika added as she savored the taste of her Oreo Cookies N Cream Malt. "Ooh, Wee, this is good."

"Yeah, my German Chocolate is good too. It is almost sinful to be enjoying this. Oh, my gosh, that looks like Andre's mother," noticed Arteah.

"Andre who?" asked Sherika.

"You know! Andre Patterson's mother is coming up the way," replied Arteah.

Mrs. Patterson looked in the window as she walked by. Arteah stood up and waved to get her attention. Mrs. Patterson stopped and waved. Immediately, Arteah went outside to greet her.

"Hi, Mrs. Patterson. Remember me?" asked Arteah.

"Of course I do, Arteah McMorris. You graduated with my son and your grandmother goes to my church," said Mrs. Patterson.

"Yes, Ma'am," Arteah said.

"Arteah, have you talked to Andre lately? He told me you came to U of I when he was drafted," inquired Mrs. Patterson.

"He told you that, Mrs. Patterson?" she said with surprise.

"Andre said he could not believe he ran into you at a club," added Mrs. Patterson. "Baby, Let's go inside; it is getting too nippy out here."

"Ok, my girlfriend, Sherika is devouring her malt," warned Arteah.

As they approached the table, Arteah said, "Sherika, this is Mrs. Patterson, Andre's mother. Andre and I went to high school together. Mrs. Patterson, Sherika and I went to Illinois State together," Arteah politely introduced the two.

They all sat at a table. Again, Andre's mom asked Arteah when was the last time she talked to her son.

"Mrs. Patterson, I have not talked to Andre since April. I guess we have both been busy, living different lives. I am teaching, and I am sure he is busy adjusting to NFL life. So how is he?" inquired Arteah.

Boastingly, Mrs. Patterson conveyed to Arteah and Sherika that so much had happened since draft day.

"It's been so exciting for him. Andre officially signed with the Tennessee Sphinx, plus a great signing bonus. He went through training camp this summer, which he said was quite challenging, but his new friend and roommate, Joe Jackson has helped him mentally stay focused. They must be close friends, because Andre speaks so highly of him. Joe is very much into the church, and he is from Texas. They often joke about his southern accent."

"What position does his roommate play?" Arteah asked.

"Quarterback. Arteah, Andre has been doing really well as a rookie. The commentators say he is adjusting very well and is very charismatic. In fact, he has been getting lots of calls to do commercials," his mother informed.

"Already?" Arteah surprisingly reacted.

"A third of the season is over. It is not like basketball. They only play one game a week," said Mrs. Patterson.

"So, I'm sure you go to all the games, then?" asked Arteah.

"As many as I can. You know Andre is thinking of buying a home in Tennessee," replied Mrs. Patterson.

"Tennessee? So Andre knows that is where he'd like to permanently live?" asked Arteah.

"Well, the people of the town really appreciate him there. You know, you should call him; he'd be glad to hear from you," suggested Ms. Patterson.

As Mrs. Patterson opened her pocketbook to pull out her phone book to find Andre's new number, Arteah could not believe Andre's mother wanted her to keep in touch with her son. She smiled, thinking to herself, 'I wonder does she know what a whore her son is. I wonder does she know her baby is the most suave of the whores. That it is a shame for somebody to be that handsome, talented and whorish without remorse. But then again, he is single to mingle.'

"Here's the number. Call Andre. He needs an old friend like you in his life," Mrs. Patterson expressed her feeling to the young lady.

"What?"

"That's right, baby. My Andre needs a genuine person in his life, someone who knows him. Now make sure you call him real soon too. Arteah, I've gotta go before it gets too dark out," Mrs. Patterson said as she began to exit.

"Yes, Ma'am. It is great seeing you. Take care," Arteah sweetly remarked as she hugged Mrs. Patterson goodbye.

Sherika gave an inquisitive look at Arteah after Mrs. Patterson left. "What was all of that about? You've been holding back info."

"What are you talking about?" smirked Arteah.

"Don't play me crazy, Art. It sounds like you and this Andre guy had something going on. True?" asked Sherika.

"Not exactly," Arteah evasively responded.

"Don't play the Bill Clinton on me. Did you and Andre have sexual relations?" Sherika rephrased her question.

"Depends on what you call sexual relations," stated Arteah with wit.

"Sex?" Sherika bluntly asked.

"No, we did not have intercourse. We just had one wonderful evening. One I'll forever treasure. It was so spontaneous," expressed Arteah, as she gazed away reflecting.

"So, you didn't have sex with that fine football player. Now, I myself, would have at least tested the waters. He might not can screw. Then, you would know if you are wasting your time. Just because those athletes are big does not mean they can burst a grape. OK?!" informed Sherika.

Arteah burst into laughter. "Where in the hell did you get that expression from?" asked Arteah.

"I don't know, but it's true. So what are his measurements? Sherika asked, wanting more insight.

"6'4", 230 pounds chiseled, 4% body fat, full moon looking buttocks," Arteah described.

"Alright, Alright," Sherika shook her head in disbelief.

"I get the picture. So are you going to call? By the way you were looking at his mother when she suggested you call, you looked hesitant."

"Sherika, I do like Andre. Hell, I'd probably fell in love with him the night he whispered beautiful words in my ear like, 'You have legs of a stallion, and don't ever de-size these,'" Arteah said.

"De-size what?" interjected Sherika.

"My balloons, you crazy girl."

"Balloons?"

"Yes, my perky, vivacious balloons."

Sherika laughed hysterically.

"And you think I'm crazy; you are far out…to Pluto," added Sherika.

"Serious, I like him. He's a homeboy. I understand him, maybe too well. We had a deep discussion on life. He thinks I'll become a professor one day over the African American Studies Department at Harvard. I feel connected to him in an endearing way, and we did not have sex. Now that's peculiar. He's dangerous too. I can't be dealing with a man who enjoys casual sex and doesn't mind being blunt about where he is in life. To be honest, I'm glad I did not let him 'burst the grape.' I'd probably turn into one of those psycho women, hiring hit men to bump him off for causing mental insanity. I am not one of those women who can call it what it is. 'This has been a good fuck; see you when I see you.' I'm one of those women who'd say, 'I thought this meant something to you by the way you looked into my eyes and touched me.' Sherika, there is nothing worse than dealing with a 'I'll see you when I see you type of man, when I know I am a 'See you in Paris' type of woman," Arteah explained.

"Oh my! I hear you, girl," added Sherika. "But are you going to call him?"

"I will call to say what's up and wish him well and that is it," Arteah firmly stated.

"You're done?" asked Sherika.

"Yeah, it's mostly melted away," responded Arteah.

They threw away their trash and headed home.

Chapter 4

"Man, that was an awesome game," Joe shouted!

"Hell yeah. We kicked much ass, didn't we," added Andre.

"Only God knows; we both are dynamic rookies. Simply amazing," Joe said.

"Especially when coach put you in the game after half time. You threw the perfect pass to me, and I ran it straight into the in zone. Touchdown, baby! Since you're doing so good at your position, I think they're going to give you more PT," remarked Andre.

"That would be a blessing to prove myself as a rookie quarterback. I know with God's help, he makes all things possible. To God be the glory," expressed Joe.

"I hear you man. That's cool, man. You are religious and all. Maybe one day, I'll be that eloquent with a southern twang. Joe, you know, you can have a lot of women just falling at your feet, but you barely hang with the fellows. I'm not trying to get you "out of there." Don't take this in a homosexual manner, but you are good looking or shall I say handsome. Let me introduce you to some of the finest women the mighty good God has ever landscaped- women with red mountains or women with white sand dunes. Whatever your desire, God has supplied us, his children with. God wants us to be pleased. Tomorrow is our day off. We had a long, yet victorious game. Let's treat ourselves. 'The Work Hard. Play Hard' motto is what we live for. Let's roll out of here," suggested Andre.

"Andre, I'm gonna have to pass. I need to call home. Ma left a message. One of the religious magazines wants me to do an article to encourage young people in the church," informed Joe.

"Joe, man, that's amazing. I never get offers like that. Well, alright. I'll see you later," Andre said.

That evening, Andre headed straight for the strip club. He found much pleasure in watching the dancing of pretty women from across the world, and they all gravitated towards the NFL player. The young women winked, batted long lashes, and imposed seductive gestures towards Andre. In fact, that was an everyday occurrence for him when he went out, and he enjoyed it. It was total ego stroking, making him feel like he was in Baskin Robbins with 31 flavors to choose from, with chocolate being his favorite.

Back at their townhouse, Joe found out the details of the upcoming interview from his mother. Mrs. Jackson had met one of the writers of *Religious Expressions* at a recent church convention in Dallas. The writer followed the draft and thought Joe was very humble in his interview on draft day. He felt Joe could be an exceptional role model for other student athletes to follow.

In so many ways, Andre and Joe were alike, yet opposites. They both had passions. Joe had a passion for religion, and Andre had a passion for women. While Joe was collecting his thoughts through meditation, the telephone rang.

""Hello, may I speak to Andre?"

"He is not here. May I take a message?" Joe politely asked.

"Tell him Arteah…Arteah McMorris called from Chicago. I went to junior and high school with him. I'm certain someone has to refresh his memory. He meets so many women. Whom am I speaking with?" she curiously asked.

"I'm his roommate, Joe."

"Oh, I've heard a lot about you," she said.

"From who? May I ask ma'am?" he inquired.

"I know Andre's mom. She told me Andre had a very church going roommate that played quarterback. Is that true? Arteah asked.

"Church going huh. I never view myself like that. I'm just blessed, and I do not mind sharing it with the world that all my success is due to God's goodness and my obedience to his word."

"I hear you. So how do you like Andre for a roommate?" she asked.

"He's a hectic guy, yet I respect him. He is an explosive wide receiver," discussed Joe.

"Joe, you are so polite in your description. Yeah, he's an excellent athlete, but let's be truthful, Andre has a long way to go towards gentleman hood," quipped Arteah.

"I don't know what you mean," Joe said.

"You'll see…so when do you think he'll return home?" asked Arteah.

"I can't say, but I will tell him you called. Does he have your number?" Joe asked.

"I'll tell you what. I'll be up grading papers, so I will try to call back much later. It's a pleasure to talk to you Joe," expressed Arteah.

"My pleasure," Joe responded.

"Ok. I'll call back. Bye."

Joe hung up. Joe thought his talk with Andre's old classmate was very conversational. He was not accustomed to Andre's female friends being so polite on the telephone. In fact, most of the women that called for Andre seemed quite rude and blunt. Joe was so accustomed to hearing harsh, abrasive voices such as "Dre dere?" From what Joe could gather from just her voice, Arteah cared for Andre like a brother.

Joe pondered that Arteah could be older than Andre; she sounded more mature than Andre.

As the phone call went further from Joe's mind, he starting thinking about finding a special lady. He secretly desired commitment and intimacy. He wanted a respectable relationship to be of honor in society. He desired a woman with virtue and a noble past. Joe would not dare consider the scene of women his roommate hung out with to be his girlfriend. Not a one. Not even from his 31 flavors. Joe fell asleep, listening to his latest Amy Grant CD.

It was 11:30 p.m. as Andre unlocked the door to their rented townhouse, two seductively dressed women snickered and pulled on Andre's clothes and rubbed their fingers through his head. Andre was starring at them both as he said, "Welcome to my world. Ladies, let your minds go free, because you are now with me. Me! How sexy am I, sweet peas? Tell big daddy how sexy he is?"

"Big daddy, Dre. You are sexy," the two women purred. The two women continued to giggle.

"Sweet peas, go get comfortable in my bedroom, and I'll go open up another bottle of champagne," Andre said.

Andre relaxed on the couch in the living room before opening up a new bottle of champagne. Thereafter, he looked on the caller I.D. to see who had called. He was amazed to see Arteah McMorris' name. He had not talked to her since his celebration in Champagne, Illinois in April. It was already October. Andre briefly reflected on their conversation and the way Arteah looked that night.

"Dre, we are waiting for you! Hurry and bring that champagne," yelled one of the frisky women.

Andre immediately snapped Arteah out of his mind and tended to the women in his bed.

The night passed peacefully for Joe. He slept deeply as Andre did not get any rest, yet pleasures. Out of respect for his roommate, Andre always ensured his company was gone before Joe awoke, so that the roommates could communicate without outside influence.

By sunlight, Joe and Andre were in the living room, looking at tapes of plays, observing competitors. What was amazing about Andre is that he could burn a nightly and a daily candle with seemingly ease. In addition, nothing could affect his performance on the field. Andre had fire energy.

"Aren't you tired, Andre?"

"No, man. You know I'm used to burning the midnight oil, but I'll rest later on."

"Oh, I almost forgot. A girl named Arteah McMorris called last night for you," remembered Joe.

"I saw it on the caller I.D."

"She sounded really nice. She was very polite," added Joe.

"Yeah, that's Arteah; she's very sweet and loving, yet crazy and exciting."

"So you two date or used to date?" Joe searched.

"Let's just say we shared a dear moment in time together as friends," answered Andre.

"Did you?"

"Naw, man. Arteah's different. That's my home girl. She treats everybody like they are the most important person in the world, not because someone makes more or less money than somebody else. That's what makes her so special. You might get a chance to meet her if she's not pissed off at me for not keeping in touch. If fact, after I lie down for a good sleep, I will give her a call," Andre shared.

Joe and Andre continued to discuss plays. Both were committed to disciplining themselves to stay on top of their game. Some hours had passed and the long night had started catching up with Andre. He started nodding.

"Dre, you need to get some rest," insisted Joe.

"I think you're right," confirmed Andre.

With zapped energy, Andre made it to his bed and finally crashed, while Joe went out to run errands.

After several hours of deep sleep, he awoke knowing he had to talk to Arteah. He was certain she was disappointed in him. After all, he had not contacted her since he made the move to Tennessee. In fact, they had not spoken since he last saw her, since that very intimate moment. He sensed that Arteah would feel those special moments meant nothing to him. He felt Arteah was overjoyed, thanking herself the two did not have intercourse.

The reality was Andre had been busy, quite overwhelmed with the adjustment to the NFL lifestyle. It was not that he did not think of picking up the phone to say hello. It was just his reality. Every time he attempted to call her, he would get distracted. He felt he had no choice but to pay attention to who was in his face. Yet he knew his behavior was unjustifiable. Andre realized he could have at least invited her to a game or two. He could have at least remembered her birthday, yet he had been so occupied. He knew Arteah remembered everything, from birthdays to even the day they graduated from Dunbar Senior High School. He knew calling her was long overdue. Finally, he dialed her number.

"Hi this is Art. I've stepped out for a brief moment. Will be back around 5. Leave a message and remember to enjoy every moment-Bye!" played her voice mail.

It was 4:45 p.m., and he thought it would be better if he talked to her, not her machine first. He knew he was in the doghouse. She'd probably not return his call if he left a message.

Andre reflected that it was just like Arteah to specialize most messages. In junior high, Arteah would bring candy and green popcorn every St. Patrick's Day and rainbow colored eggs during Easter Celebrations. Fifteen minutes passed quickly before he attempted to redial.

"Hello," greeted Arteah.

"Hey, this is Andre."

"Andre who," asked Arteah.

"Patterson. Andre Patterson."

Art starts to laugh. "Oh, my stranger friend!! What's up, you shameless creature," she greeted.

"Nothing much. I apologize for not keeping in touch," addressed Andre.

"Oh, you don't have to apologize for being you. So how is NFL living? I see Tennessee is doing pretty well," added Arteah.

"I'm having a good time," stated Andre.

Andre could tell Arteah was somewhat cold in her conversation, yet she was still courteous. He wondered how he could pick up where they finished in Champaign with such verbal and physical intensity for one another. What could he expect? She knew he was a fucking machine on automatic, living by his 'spiritec' philosophy.

The truth was he wanted to preserve Arteah until he was ready to change his 'spiritec' philosophy. At least he knew where he was in life. At least he could be honest with himself and not lead her on like so many married men in the NFL had led their wives along. He did not want to put her through any high drama catfights with other women and impose emotional insecurities that he so often saw in the most beautiful women. She did not deserve to see him in this phase of his life, a phase that one day he knew would be behind him.

"You know, I saw your mom and somehow she persuaded me to call. She said you needed an old friend like me, but I think you are doing just fine. The more I think about life, it's like the quote says, 'No permanent friends, no permanent enemies, just permanent teachers!' Hey after all I am a teacher," Arteah expressed.

"So how are you adjusting to the classroom?" asked Andre.

"Good, I love the kids, but I do feel quite motherly in this position. I'm still young you know. I still have plenty of wild dreams to fulfill. You know who much I love to travel and explore."

Andre immediately thought of asking her to visit Tennessee, to attend a game.

"Art, I know I have been an inconsiderate friend, but I'd love for you to come to Tennessee, to come to my game, to simply enjoy yourself."

"That's kind of you, Dre, but you don't have to over-extend your schedule to accommodate me," said Arteah.

"I am not over-extending my schedule. It's my pleasure."

"Oh, we both know you really enjoy pleasures," remarked Arteah.

"Please come," begged Andre.

"Cum?" Art laughed.

"You know what I mean. You can stay at my place," suggested Andre.

"No, I don't think so, if I come. I insist on staying at the hotel. I don't want to stay at the SPIRITEC house. I will visit it, but I can not stay there," warned Arteah.

"Ok, if you insist. As long as you come and visit," he said delightfully. "Great. My agent will call you with all of the flight and hotel arrangement. I will be practicing; and it maybe hard to catch up with me, but I will see you Friday and do not change your mind."

"Ok," accepted Art. "I'll see you Friday."

They said their goodbyes, both looking forward to an interesting, upcoming weekend.

Chapter 5

Sherika took Arteah to the airport, and wished her close friend a fun time. Arteah was met in Nashville by Andre's agent, holding a sign with her name on it. He then took her to the hotel where she settled in. Arteah was extremely excited about her visit. More than seeing her old classmate, Andre, she was anxious to see Tennessee, a place she had never visited before. She had heard that there were caves in the state. It was the home of Elvis and Oprah attended Tennessee State University.

As she looked at the view of Nashville, the phone rang in her room. She rushed to pick it up.

"Hello?" Arteah greeted.

"Art! This is Dre. Glad you made it in. I hope you did not have any problems on your way in," inquired Andre.

"No, I didn't. Anthony was there to pick me up in the baggage claim area. He was so nice to me," Arteah responded.

"Yeah, he's a cool guy. Listen Art, I am going to send my roommate, Joe, to come pick you up for dinner, because I have to do a feature interview with one of the Sports Magazines. I'll tell him to be there around 6:45 p.m. That'll give you time to relax a bit before you get ready. Is that ok?"

"Yeah, sure. I'll be ready. What's your roommates name again?" asked Arteah.

"Joe Jackson. He is a nice guy too, so don't worry," assured Andre.

"Ok. I guess this means I will see you at the restaurant. Bye," said Arteah.

Arteah immediately made a long distance call to Sherika's cellular phone.

"Sherika! Help! I'm here in Tennessee. I just got through talking to Andre. I'll see him for dinner tonight, but I don't have anything proper to wear. I packed all wrong. I think I brought too many casual clothes. What was I thinking," panicked Arteah.

"Art, I thought this guy is just an old classmate who enjoyed one special moment with you. He invited you to a game, because he feels guilty that he has not kept in contact," Sherika asserts.

"Yeah, yeah, I know. What am I even doing here? You should have come with me, to help me keep my cool," vented Arteah.

"You do not need me there. You have it all together, but you don't know you have it all together. I know you packed either the cute red cocktail dress or that sizzling, sexy, winter white, leather Capri pants outfit. So don't give me that bullshit about you not having anything to wear. Didn't you pack them?" demanded Sherika.

"Yeah, I packed both of them. I'll figure it out. I can't believe I got off the airplane and lost my mind. I don't know what I am expecting from this visit, if anything," Arteah whined.

"I think you like this guy more than you lead on. You are just scared of rejection, but who in the hell is not scared of that.

Sure, he's fine. He's a millionaire, but this has nothing to do with whether or not he can fuck or could be an amazing, faithful man. Keep that in mind. So when you start feeling insecure, remember you deserve good sex and a pedestal from him. If he can't give you both, then that fine, sculptured body doesn't mean a damned thing. He's just a pin-up poster, and the millions of dollars won't even pacify your aching, yearning body and emotions," Sherika warned.

"I know," chuckled Arteah. "See this is the reason you are my dearest friend. You are there for me in so many ways. Thanks girl. It'll be 6:45 before I know it, and I need to relax and enjoy my getaway. I'll call you later."

"Ok, Art. Let me know how you mesmerize him and all his cute friends," Sherika said with excitement.

"You know you are bizarre. What interest would I have in his friends? Ok, I'll finally admit. I'm crazy about Andre, and I have been for some time. That's all I need is Andre trying to pass me off to his friends, giving me away without remorse or thought. I think this would be a reason to leave the country and escape to Africa and live with wild monkeys, because I would feel like one, you know," bluntly remarked Arteah.

"Call me later, Art," Sherika said.

"Bye, and thanks again," Arteah said, ending the conversation.

Arteah relaxed, showered, then dressed herself. Her nails and hair were highly refined. For the first time in a while, she had hours to just focus on herself. She had pampering time in a five star hotel with a balcony, overlooking a wonderful metropolitan, southern city. She was comfortable with her own company.

Eventually, her anxieties had left her. She knew the white leather pantsuit would be the perfect allure.

While she was waiting, watching videos on television, she heard a knock at the door. Turning down the volume on the remote control, she went to the door and asked,

"Who is it?"

"Joe Jackson. I'm here to pick up Arteah McMorris."

"One moment," as Arteah unlocked the door.

"Hello, I am Andre's roommate. Are you ready?" asked Joe.

"Come in. I just need to lock the balcony and get my purse. I remember talking to you on the telephone. Do you remember me?" asked Arteah.

"Uhm, yes, ma'am. I remember you. You were very polite and conversational over the telephone," Joe responded.

"Joe, you do not have to call me ma'am. It makes me feel old. It's enough students have to call me Ms. McMorris," Arteah informs.

"Well, uhm, it is just out of respect," assured Joe Jackson.

"So, I assume you are a teacher?"

"Yes, I teach high school-social studies," Arteah replied.

"I really admire and respect you for your position. It is not easy being a teacher nowadays. I mean our society depends on you and other teachers to inspire young minds and not just to instruct. You have to have that extra something to inspire," Joe added.

"Yeah, I guess you're right. It's a gift from God. I am a natural teacher. I really don't have to work hard at teaching and inspiring students to do things. However, I am at a decent school. Don't get me wrong; I have some co-workers who deal with students with serious behavioral problems and other mental disabilities, such as Attention Deficiency Disorders in one class. Imagine a few students in one class showing all of the signs of ADD and their parents do not want to come to terms with the reality that their children may need medication," discussed Arteah.

Joe was inquisitive about Arteah's life as an educator. What fascinated him was her poise and intellect, but he did not want to irritate her with teacher questions, so he tried to change the subject as they drove to the restaurant to meet Andre.

"Have you been to Tennessee before?" inquired Joe.

"No, this is my first time. Do you like it here?" asked Arteah.

"Tennessee is a beautiful piece of land, but of course I miss Texas. The people are very nice here, and it is a lot to see and explore," Joe shared, looking at her out of the corner of his right eye.

"Yeah, I hear they have caves here," Arteah said.

"They do. Maybe, Andre, one day, can get a chance to show you the caves and other tourist attractions in the area. I take it you are looking forward to seeing Andre?" inquired Joe.

Arteah modestly said, "It is always nice to see an old friend. We went to high school together, and we are just old acquaintances reacquainting. I am proud of his accomplishments. I'm sure all of our old classmates are too."

"Arteah, your accomplishments are stellar in the rarest light," Joe expressed.

"Why, thank you, Joe. Aren't you gracious? Most people do not value teachers the way they value athletes. Your thoughts are really sweet and dear. Andre told me you were really nice, but he did not say how nice," Arteah revealed.

"We are here at the restaurant, now," Joe alerted.

He parked the car, got out of the car and opened the door for Arteah. Joe took a good glance at her without rudely staring. He noticed she possessed an earthly, angelic charm. She looked beautiful. He wondered how one woman got packaged so well- the charm, sense of humor, intelligence, professionalism, class, and striking features. What was his roommate thinking, passing up an opportunity of a lifetime. Perhaps she was too much for Andre.

As they walked into the seafood restaurant, Andre was right at the door to greet them both. They had reservations for 7:30.

"Art, my main girl," Andre greeted with a warm, long hug.

"Hi," she embraced him in return.

"I am so glad you are here; it's an amazing town," expressed Andre. "Oh man, you know I did not forget about you. Thanks for picking her up. I owe you big time."

"No problem at all. Anytime," Joe responded.

"So are you staying for dinner, Joe," asked Arteah.

"Yeah, man," invited Andre.

"Thanks, but I have some errands to run," Joe said.

"So when will I hear about both of your NFL stories, wild parties, and all. An inquiring mind wants to know," joked Arteah.

"We'll stop by our place. Joe, are you going to be in around 10? I took out photos a reporter took of the team, plus I dug out our old high school year book," said Andre.

"No, you are not pulling out that old, black and white mug shot from high school. That yearbook was so low budget. It's embarrassing," pleaded Arteah.

"Yes, I'll be home around 10. I'd enjoy seeing those pictures," laughed Joe.

Joe gave Andre a masculine handshake/hug, and extended his hand to Arteah. Sincerely, she reached to hug him and said, "Thanks for your hospitality, and for making me feel wonderful."

The hostess finally seated Arteah and Andre for dinner, and Joe left. As Joe drove away, he could not help but think about his encounter with this exciting woman. Her voice echoed in his ears the word, 'for making me feel wonderful.' Then, all he could think was what a fortunate man his roommate was, to be able to have intimate dinner with a woman like Arteah.

"That lucky rascal," he mumbled.

He tended to all of his errands.

"Dre, I can't decide. I haven't had cake in a while. Ice crème-yes, but chocolate mouse cake and especially cheesecake?" she confessed.

"I tell you what. I will get the chocolate mouse cake, and you get the cheesecake. Then you can taste both," suggested Andre.

"Oh I thought we were going to share our slice. So many calories?" informed Arteah.

"Well, whatever you don't eat, you can have for the rest of the weekend," Andre pointed out.

"Yeah, you're right. I guess with desserts, I am just as greedy and indecisive as you are when it comes to women," Arteah joked.

"What? Aren't you a trip? I knew you were not going to let me off the hook that easy. I knew it," said Andre.

"What hook? What are you talking about?" she naively replied.

"Art, you are too classy to come out and just say, "Why the fuck haven't you called me in all this Goddamned time? And we are supposed to be home skillets? I know that is what you are thinking?" Andre expressed frankly.

"Home Skillet," she laughed. "No, Dre. I know what you are; I realize that you are a man of *active* extremes on and off the field."

"There you go again with all of these double meanings," interjected Andre.

"Why are you getting so offended? Boy, I am just joking," Arteah conversed.

Arteah ate a third of her cheesecake and a mouthful taste of Andre's chocolate mouse cake.

"Delicious! I'd better take the rest to go," said Arteah.

The waitress graciously boxed the cheesecake, and Andre took care of the bill.

Andre drove to the riverfront on 1st Street. The two took a brief walk in the brisk weather, while Joe was returning home from running errands. As Joe sat down to watch television, he noticed a photo album on the coffee table. He knew the album must be his roommate's high school memory book. Curiously, he glanced at the pictures. He noticed Arteah was hugging on a young man, and it was not his roommate. As he studied the picture, he noticed it was an affectionate hug, since the male student had his hands on Arteah's rear end. As he turned the page of the photo album, he saw a close up shot of Arteah photographed alone near red lockers. The picture captured her innocent eyes and winning smile. This one particular picture captivated Joe. As he browsed through the other pictures, he constantly returned to the picture of Arteah by the locker.

Seeing her high school pictures was like feeling her history. Joe felt like he was familiar with her; he felt like he knew what she needed. At first, he assumed Andre and Arteah had a relationship or that they were an item in high school at some point. However, the pictures convinced him differently. There was not one picture of them together. It appeared they were really just old classmate acquaintances. 'Why am I so taken by this woman?' Joe thought. 'I think it is the way she looked at me. Then again, she looked at Andre the same way. Ok, she just has an alluring aura.'

As Joe's mind continued to wonder, Andre and Arteah walked into the townhouse laughing.

"Hey, man, I see you've been checking out the pictures," Andre said.

"Yes. It looks like you two had a good time in high school," Joe noted.

"We did, wouldn't you say, Art?" Andre asked.

"Yes, high school was naturally fun. College was naturally exciting. What I find in my post-college era is that I have to work to ensure my life is fun and exciting," responded Arteah.

Andre ensured Arteah was comfortable at his place. He gave her a tour of their home. Joe enjoyed Arteah's company, particularly her perspectives on life. Joe was quite inquisitive, yet he tried to remain aloof. He tried to conceal his fascination with his roommate high school acquaintance. Joe thought it was showing in his eyes, his deep admiration for Arteah. 'Maybe Andre can tell I like her,' Joe thought.

"Well, you two, I am going to bed," Joe stated as he began exiting the living room.

"So early, Joe. I am enjoying your company so much. I love to hear you talk. Your Texas accent is so unique and warming to my ears," Arteah expressed.

"Thanks, but I must get my sleep; I'm an early riser," informed Joe.

"Ok man. Good night," responded Andre.

Joe went to his bedroom thinking not only was Miss Arteah McMorris fascinating, she was most sensuous and delightful. She knew what to say and how to say it. Andre and Arteah talked for another hour, before Andre drove her back to her hotel. Arteah was too exhausted to call her girl friend to fill her in on the details of her first night in Tennessee.

Chapter 6

Sunday, game day, had arrived in Nashville. Andre had introduced Arteah to his head coach's wife. She had shown Arteah and some of the other guest a delightful, time, while Andre, Joe and the rest of the Nashville team prepared for the big game. Arteah had never been to a NFL game. She had only attended high school and college games. She was now sitting on the 50 yard line in a newly built stadium. She was in one of the best seats in the stadium, elated at the magnitude of NFL excitement. Playoffs were a game away and the momentum was peaking, because the Nashville Sphinx had ensured their spot in the playoffs.

Kick off was at noon. She looked through her binoculars to see close-ups of Andre and the rest of the team. The opposing team had no chance of making it to the playoffs. They were not even a wild card team. Nashville's goal was to play it safe after half time to prevent unnecessary injuries of top players; nevertheless, New Orleans was fighting for dignity. They wanted to end with a win, even though the majority of the season was filled with frustrating losses.

New Orleans offense pushed to score first within the first five minutes, but Nashville answered with a touchdown and a field goal. Soon thereafter, a Nashville linebacker intercepted New Orlean's top wide receiver. Nashville's head coach ran the unexpected play at the 30 yard line. The crowd thought running back, #10, was going to rush, but quarterback Jackson threw to wide receiver, #32 Andre Patterson. Catching the football, Andre headed straight to the in zone. Touchdown. The crowd went wild. Andre almost gestured an in zone dance. This play had taken the last ounce of hope out of New Orleans. New Orleans could not hold the explosive creative offense. The game went as expected, Nashville over New Orleans 32-7.

Arteah took in the atmosphere. The fans were most exciting. She took lots of pictures, even of the bizarre fans with painted faces. She did not understand everything that was happening play for play on the field, but she definitely knew what a stellar win was.

Janet led her and the rest of the guests to where the players would come out of the locker room. Fans, in particular, young kids, had their pen, paper, and footballs ready to hopefully get autographs. There were plenty of beautiful women waiting also; she blended in well with the rest of the young women. The winning team finally began to come out of the locker room. They had transformed to look like top business executives in tailored suites. Some even wore designer shades. Arteah noticed Joe, Andre's roommate. She called him, but she realized twenty other people were calling his name too. Most were blonde, striking women who looked like supermodels. One woman even wore a cowboy hat and western wear to get his attention since she learned Joe was from Texas.

Arteah exhausted herself from calling his name and mellowed herself to simply watching the phenomenal. Arteah could see the constant temptations any man would have being in such a position, where he had everything going for himself-youth, fulfilled dreams, gladiator body, and money. Arteah, for the first time could understand why so many women waited patiently for their seemingly perfect man.

"Why? The excitement. The power. The fear of living a common life. The fear of mediocre living," she mumbled to herself.

She knew reporters may come to the 'hood to do a story on poverty and "Lifestyles of the Rich and Famous" would perhaps do a story on athletes and actors, but no one would ever give a pedestal to common living, unless the interviewers were making money somehow. Arteah knew society needed lukewarm water, but people are mostly fascinated by extremes.

"Arteah," shouted Joe.

She snapped out of her over analyzing trance.

"Hey, Joe," she yelled back.

As he made his way over to her, she saw Andre finally coming out of the locker room. Joe hugged her, and Arteah told him, "Good game. Wow, are you talented? Did your parents make it to the game to see you lead the team to victory?"

"No, they couldn't make it. It was too much going on at church this Sunday but I'm sure they taped it," expressed Joe.

"That's nice. Andre should be out now," informed Joe.

"I saw him. He is signing autographs and talking to admirers," noticed Arteah.

"Arteah, to me, fans are fans, nothing more, nothing less," lastly remarked Joe as he continued to make his way out of the stadium. Andre finally forced himself a loose from his fans. Some were obviously more than fans. His two "sweet peas" were waiting on him. He certainly did not give them tickets to the game. The woman couple expected to leave with Andre. A little uptight, Andre finally made his way to greet Arteah.

"Did you enjoy yourself?" asked Andre.

"Yes, the fans are hysterical."

"I know," agreed Andre.

"Good game! I saw you run for that touchdown," Arteah commented.

"Yeah, Joe threw a sweet pass, no doubt. Are you ready to go?" asked Andre.

"Yea, sure," replied Arteah.

"Oh, it's like that? Who is this bitch? You couldn't be satisfied with us," yelled the two women.

Andre was in disbelief, because some children had heard them, and the two had called Arteah a bitch. Arteah turned around to see. She could not believe strangers called her a bitch. She went into a state of shock. Arteah knew she did not come to vacation in Tennessee to end up being called a bitch by strangers.

Arteah calmly said, "Look, I don't know what the relationship you two have with Andre, but I am no bitch, bitch! I do not appreciate being addressed like that, bitches."

One of the girls reached for Arteah, and Andre suddenly grabbed her hand. Profanity from the obnoxious women continued until security escorted them out. As Andre and Arteah made it to the car, Arteah had never been so silent, yet Andre knew in time she would explode. All he could do was drive and wait. Riding for ten minutes, Arteah said, "I need to go back to my hotel, so I can get the earliest flight out, instead of leaving tomorrow, thank you."

Andre briefed, "I'm sorry, Art. I had no control over that situation. I did not invite them to the game. I had no idea they would be there."

"Stop it. Just stop it!! I don't have to hear this pathetic line of reasoning. One day you are going to get someone killed with the road you're going down if not your self. You just don't get it. You can not play with women's emotions to pursue your selfish pleasures. More and more, I see you for who you are. You are an addict, not a drug addict, not even an alcoholic addict, but a pleasure addict. I have nothing else to say, Andre. Nothing!"

Arteah and Andre made it back to the hotel.

"Thank you, Andre for the invitation. I have enjoyed my stay, but it time for me to go," she quipped.

Andre knew there would not be any night walks, passionate kisses, and snuggling with his long time friend. He did not need sex from her. He desired understanding from her. She understood him better than he understood himself. He, inconsiderately, wanted her to tolerate his nature until he was ready to make changes. Yet he knew toleration was not in her nature, maybe for her students, but not toleration for his situation.

"Art, I only want to ask one thing of you? Will you stay the night and just relax. Call up the massage therapist, enjoy the hotel before I insist on taking you to the airport in the morning."

"Maybe...Alright, but I want time to myself," warned Arteah.

"I am really sorry; I put you in harms way. Forgive me," expressed Andre.

"No grudges. After all, you are not my husband, nor my man. I just know you, that's all," Arteah said.

"So the night we spent together in Champaign did not mean anything to you? asked Andre.

"So did the nights you probably spent with those two women mean anything to you?" asked Arteah.

"You just won't quit. You have no mercy. None, but I still adore you only," remarked Andre.

"Well, thank you. I'll see you at noon for check out," said Arteah.

Andre kissed her on the cheek and said goodbye.

Arteah talked to the concierge about hotel activities and dining, before returning to her room to shower. She then put on her strapless satin, cocktail dress, make-up, and the sexiest heels, and headed to dinner at the steakhouse downstairs. The hostess seated her, and asked if she would be dining alone.

"Yes, I am dining alone, thank you," Arteah eloquently answered.

She ordered red wine before her dinner. She took notice of the ambiance of the restaurant. She observed the jazz quartet in the corner. The small group consisted of a drummer, pianist, bassist and eccentric looking trumpet player. The music sounded serene, yet mysteriously seductive to Arteah's ears. Other dining guests were coupled off and the bar area consisted mostly of white collared looking men. Her food arrived, and she gracefully indulged.

Later in the evening, a man from the bar came over to her table to make acquaintance.

"I am Paul Robertson. I could not help but notice your exotic beauty from across the room."

"Why thank you. I am Arteah," she informed.

"Such a unique name. I attempted to wait until you completely finished your dinner. I insist on a dance from you," suggested the man.

"I really don't dance to that type of music."

"I insist. They are playing the ballad of ballads."

"What? Ballad?" Arteah asked, because she was confused by his accent.

"*Round Midnight,*" a ballad Miles Davis was known for performing. Let's dance," he repeatedly asked. Arteah had to accept. She danced slowly to "*Round Midnight*" as the trumpet player passionately soloed. Arteah noticed the music left her feeling romantic. The music of jazz provided the most romantic stage for seduction. They continued to dance the evening away to instrumental versions of "*Unforgettable*" and "*Almost Like Being in Love.*"

At the end of their dancing, the tall, lean man kissed her on the cheek and offered sincere thanks. They sat back at her candle lit table and talked. She discovered the distinguished gentleman was a black Frenchman, who was currently based in Toronto, and an engineer in Nashville. Paul attentively listened to every word she said. She felt it by the way he stared at her. His hazel brown eyes and pronounced cheekbones were too alluring for Arteah. She was attracted to him and the smooth accent did not help her growing arousal for him.

In their time, they walked arm in arm around the hotel and sat by the inside waterfall. Arteah noticed his conversation was so intimate, warming and affectionate, because he whispered most things in her ear. Arteah started thinking, "Hey, you can do a couple of things to my ear besides talk in it. Hey, this brother gets my brownie for Number 1: being sexy; Number 2: talking sexy, and Number 3 making me feel sexy. Oh damn! It's on!! Who gives a darn he lives in Canada. I can't remember the last time I've been seduced this creatively. It is totally in the way he makes me feel at this moment. All he has to say is…Take it off!! Take it off!!…and my clothes will disappear!"

"Arte, are you alright? Where did you go? What were you thinking? I want to know," asked Paul.

"No, you don't. I was just listening to the sounds of the waterfall," chuckled Arteah.

"I see you enjoy waterfalls. You must come to Toronto, and I will take you to the most exquisite waterfall of Niagara," Paul suggested.

"Oh, you are so nice," Arteah acknowledged.

"No, my dear, you are so nice and sweet, that I want to eat you. You are most adorable. Tell me you don't have a lover. Please tell me you don't have a lover," spoke the black Frenchman, pulling Arteah hair gently back.

Her mind wondered again. "Well, Andre is not my lover. Hell, I really don't consider him my friend. I'm his friend; he's my acquaintance, who I've grown to have deep affections for. We shared one unforgettable night together. I can now come to terms with that, especially looking at Paul and hearing his voice."

"Tell me Arte…Tell me you do not have a lover," Paul reiterated.

"No, I have acquaintances, almost too many, but no lovers," expressed Arteah.

Paul kissed her passionately as if she were his beautiful bride on wedding day. Paul made every second special. He touched her neck with deep affection. She felt weightless. She knew she could not pass up on enjoying the most seductive, romantic moment yet in her life with an old soul, yet a stranger. Paul made lover to her mind and body in Room 1224.

They awoke to a beautiful sunrise. Paul ordered breakfast in bed. He immediately took care of the bill and charged it to his room. He held her like she was his precious angel, the rarity he had been searching for. To him, she represented genuineness. She was the exotic plant that needed special care. He found his present and future in her. What a difference a night made. Paul spoon-fed her breakfast, and he quenched his appetite for her once more before having to catch an early flight back to Toronto. Paul gave her his information, all the numbers he could be reached at. She gave him her home and cellular numbers, plus an emergency number at school.

"Arte, you have given me the most precious gift I will forever cherish. I hope this is the beginning of the greatest love affair. I'll call you as soon as I can. You are an amazing kisser. You drive me crazy, Arte. Crazy, my lover," Paul expressed. He kissed her one last time.

Arteah lay in the bed, feeling bliss and serenity. She thought "What a lover. You know, I no longer want boyfriends. I only want lovers, and eventually one supreme lover to last a lifetime. Paul definitely is my supreme candidate. Oh, do I feel sexy! I must be gleaming like a fluorescent light! I did not expect this. I thought Andre would have been lying next to me last night, but Paul surpassed all expectations. I think I'm going to pick up that Miles Davis CD with *"Round Midnight"* on it when I get back to Chicago."

The phone rang.

"Art. Hi. I tried calling you last night, but you must have been downstairs. Are you about ready? I'm about 10 minutes away," Andre informed.

"Ok. I'll be ready. Just call me when you get in the lobby," Arteah said.

Arteah had not moved from her bed since Paul left. She jumped up quickly, because she had so many items to pack down. She showered and put on her Levi's Blue jean form fitting dress and high-heeled boots.

Andre soon called. When he saw Arteah, he saw her in a different light, not just the hometown friend. He knew for sure that she was the most beautiful woman he had ever known, but he did not know how to treat her that way for the rest of his life. Andre took care of the charges at the front desk, and they headed towards the airport. The two stopped at a cozy deli to eat lunch.

For the first time, Andre had more to say than Arteah. She was still in bliss land from last night. She could even hear the trumpet playing the melody of "*Round Midnight.*" Arteah just looked at Andre talk; she did not hear much.

"Can I see you if we end up playing Chicago," asked Andre.

"Yeah, holler at me, home skillet," nonchalantly replied Arteah.

"Are you Ok? You seem not your talkative self," asked Andre.

"Well, I am a little exhausted. It's been a full, surprising weekend. I'm just trying to digest it all," Arteah conveyed.

"Will you send me copies of the pictures you took? I would really appreciate it," asked Andre.

"No problem, home skillet," said Arteah.

They finished eating. Andre took her into to the airport. Some fans noticed the professional athlete. He smiled, but gave no autographs to ensure Arteah would be on time for her flight.

"For what it's worth, I know you are the most amazing, exciting, intelligent, and beautiful woman I know. I do respect you. I know I am unable to honor you like you deserve. So forgive me. You deserve the best. I do care deeply for you," Andre said, confessing his emotions.

He kissed her on the cheek and forehead, and gave her a big hug.

"Thanks for coming to visit, Art," Andre spoke gently.

"Thank you for inviting me. Take care," Arteah warmly expressed.

They kept waving goodbye as Arteah walked further and further away from him, as she walked to the gate.

Chapter 7

Joe called home, because he did not hear from his parents on game day.

"Joe, we got so busy at the church; we didn't catch your game," said Mrs. Jackson.

"Did you tape it?" inquired Joe.

"Naw, we didn't even have time to set the VCR, but you know we love you and miss you. Everybody at the church said hi, and they can't wait until you come home. When are you coming home?"

"Ma, I'm mid-season. We're in the playoffs," said Joe.

"You will be home for Christmas, right?"

"Ma, Maybe. I have been trying to get ya'll to come to Tennessee to spend some time here for at least one weekend?"

"Joe, you know that is too far for all of us to be traveling this time of year."

"Mom, I've offered to fly all of you here, but you won't come and bring the little ones," expressed Joe.

"You know they are so active with their activities at school and with the church."

"Ma, you mean just with the church. They are not involved in any school activities. They just go to school and live at the church."

"I thought I raised you better than that. Just because you are making money now, that is your money! Your daddy provides just fine for all of us. We don't need your assistance. If he can't afford the trip to Tennessee, then we can't come. I don't want him to think his son is more man than he, because you can fly all of us on an airplane now," warned his mother.

"What? Where is all of this coming from? I thought you wanted me to become something special, so I could help our family," Joe communicated.

"The family needs you home to help the little ones with their homework. We need you here to help out in the church. When was the last time you've been to church? College games were on Saturdays, but this NFL stuff makes me wonder about where your values are now. Working on the Sabbath won't lead to a prosperous life. I'm worried about you, Joe," quipped Mrs. Jackson.

"I'm fine. Tell everybody I said Hi."

"Ok, but you get home soon," demanded his mother.

Joe was so confused. He thought how could the mother who taped his games and was so supportive end up not being supportive. He rationalized that maybe the Sunday games really did bother his mother. Joe felt like he had no one to share his success with. Joe felt so alone, even though he had many fans. He knew he had thus far lived a righteous life. He was always humbled, courteous, and always gave God the praise. The words of his mother continuously played in his ear as he drifted to sleep.

Sherika picked Arteah up at the airport. Back at her place, there were flowers for her at the leasing office.

"Looks like your friend, Andre, left you flowers. Must have been a passionate weekend?" Sherika prodded. "So when you're ready to discuss details, let me know," her best friend added. Arteah read the card.

To my angel, I can't wait to kiss your lips. Stay sweet, your lover, Paul.

Arteah blushed, while possessing a reflective look in her eyes.

"Paul? Who is Paul?" asked Sherika.

"Stop being so nosey," interjected Arteah.

"I know that's not Andre's nickname. So what's the deal?"

Arteah was quite evasive. It felt like Sherika and her were reversing roles. Sherika was understood to be the extremely sexually active one, and Arteah was known for her teasing flings. Arteah had never judged her best friend. She accepted her unconditionally. Arteah settled in her apartment with her luggage and flowers.

"Ok. Ok! I met this alluring man at the hotel I was staying at. We met during dinner. He asked me to dance. We danced and...one thing led to another," informed Arteah.

"And?" asked Sherika.

"We went to sleep," Arteah laughed.

"Before the sleep part," Sherika demanded.

"Ok. Ok!! Ok!!! He seduced me, and he made love to me. My entire body shook with fulfillment, joy and happiness. My toes curled and my eyeballs went to back of my head."

"Wow. Are you serious? Wow! Now, where was Andre? I thought you two were going to dinner," asked Sherika.

"Let's say a lot happened between me getting excited to go out with my home skillet, Andre and meeting erotic, Paul," Arteah informed.

"It sounds like you had a sizzling getaway. Too sizzling. So what's up with Paul? Sherika inquired.

"I don't know. We'll see," said Arteah, unworried.

"It doesn't sound like a one night stand with him sending flowers. So, is he from Tennessee?"

"No, he was in town on business. He is actually a black Frenchman, who lives in Canada.

"I've never imagined that combination before," expressed Sherika.

"Me either, but he is so sensuous and too sexy," Arteah shouted.

Arteah smelled her flowers and began to slightly unpack.

"Sherika, I am quite exhausted. It's been a long, unbelievable weekend. I think I'm going to crash. Thanks so much for picking me up, and I will fill you in on the rest of the details later."

Sherika left, and Arteah listened to her messages. Her mother, Paul, and Andre called. Paul left a bantering message in French with the English translation. Andre left a platonic, friendly message of sincerity. Arteah was too exhausted to return anyone's message.

Chapter 8

Everything returned back to normal for Arteah at school. While she was driving home from work, her cell phone rang.

"*Bonsoir*, Arte," greeted the Frenchman.

"Paul?" inquired Arteah.

"I assumed high schools in the states are released at about 3:30, and I knew you would not be staying at work a moment later, am I right?" asked Paul.

"Definitely," Arteah agreed.

"So what did you wear that was most appealing to everyone's eyes today?"

"Oh, a fitted violet pants suit with these colorful beaded accessories, and of course high heels."

"I am so glad you realize how sexy and professional you are. What a killer combination. I'm certain I would learn everything in your class," added Paul.

"Thank you or shall I say *merci beaucoup* for the wonderful flowers, Paul."

"Arte, you are most worthy. So worthy, I must insist you come to visit Toronto and me this weekend. I promise I will take you to Niagara Falls," Paul said.

"Thank you for the offer, but I need time to regroup. I had a full and surprising weekend," Arteah told her new lover.

"The reason I prefer for our official first date to be in Toronto...Let's face it. Toronto is a little more romantic than Chicago. Don't get me wrong; I love strolling the Magnificent Mile and eating Chicago's famous Italian pizza. Let's say Canada possesses a different type of romanticism," Paul revealed.

"It just takes time to prepare for another trip," confessed Arteah.

"Arte, all I need for you to worry about is packing shoes, make-up, and sitting on the airplane. I'll take care of the rest."

"What?" Arteah asked.

"I'll make sure the limousine picks you up at your place and the driver makes sure you are on the plane. Just bring a carry on. What size are you? Never mind. My tongue memory remembers very vividly. I will pick you up at the airport, and we will begin our official date. Don't worry; you will be back in time to get plenty of rest Sunday. How about it Arte? I must see you again. You drive me crazy. I must whisper in your ears how I love the architecture and engineering of your mind. Your body just drives me crazy. Arte. Simply crazy! You are dangerous to any man who gets the opportunity to know you. Really. I mean that. You are a dangerous woman. Will you take my offer Arte?"

Arteah accepted.

Before she knew it, Friday had arrived, and she was in flight to Toronto. The whole week had been a whirlwind. In so many ways, she was going with the flow. She had her hesitations about going, and trusting her stranger lover, but Paul made her feel sexy, blissful, and fulfilled. Paul met her at the terminal with a bouquet of flowers and a French kiss.

"Thank you for coming. I promise you won't regret getting on that plane," informed Paul.

Arteah smiled with serenity in spirit. She had no expectations for the weekend, so she could not be disappointed if something went wrong. The French Canadian took her to his haven, which was outside the city. Arteah realized that Paul had down played his business efforts. His home was immaculate, almost intimidating to her. He was so refined, and his haven reflected it. He even had a French designed courtyard. Arteah was speechless. She did not know what to say.

"Are you ok, Arte," asked Paul.

"Yes. You have a beautiful home," said Arteah.

"Thanks. Let me show you where you can put your luggage. Also, I could not decide on which dress item to buy you. So I thought I'd let you pick."

As Arteah looked in the closet, she saw two gowns, three casual dresses, two pairs of slacks and designer matching shirts. She looked at the sizes.

"You guessed my size perfectly," observed Arteah.

"Actually I cheated a bit at the hotel in Tennessee. I noticed your size there," revealed Paul.

Arteah laughed.

"But there's more, my Arte. Open the drawer over there," Paul directed.

When Arteah opened the drawer, she noticed the sexiest, most expensive lingerie- laced bras, matching thong underwear, and teddies with all the tags left on them.

T.C. Beatty

"Paul, you didn't have to do this. This is too much," confessed Arteah.

"No, you deserve this and more. You are supposed to be lit up and dazzling. See, I've met a lot of women, but you are the rarity. Your internal beauty makes me want to give you all I have. All of me," expressed Paul. She gave him a hug and said thanks.

"I'll start your bath water, so you can change. Wear one of the gowns. We're going to dinner and dancing," Paul informed his new interest.

"Alright, Paul," said Arteah.

She sat for a while in pure bliss. It was her true fantasy and reality blended together. She had to pinch herself. She had always envisioned special moments with a wonderful man, but to have her reality fulfilled was overwhelming. Paul was romantic and into pleasing her.

She bathed in rose pedals, while listening to Miles Davis as she transformed into a goddess of the night. She wore her hair up with curls cascading around her face. When she tried to come out of her room, she noticed the door would not open. She tried to open it, but it would not open. She knocked on it and cutely called Paul's name.

"Paul? Paul? The door won't open, sweetie," she said.

Paul did not answer. The silence of Paul worried her, making her instantly paranoid.

"Paul?" she started bamming. "The door won't open."

She knocked most aggressively.

"Open the door. What's going on? There must be a lock on the other side. Open the door."

Paranoia began to marinate on her mind. The longest three minutes of her life had passed. She went to look for the phone across the room. There was no phone. Fear began to set in. The only window was the thick window in the bathroom. Tears began to water Arteah's face.

"Oh my God! What the hell have I gotten myself into? I knew this was too good to be true, meeting Paul. He's too perfect. I knew it. At least with Andre, I know him. I know his mamma. I know the way he thinks. This shit isn't cute, being locked up in this room. I hope this isn't some French, kinky crap, 'cause it isn't cute," she thought.

She ran to the door again, banging on it with fearless aggression.

"Open the damn door! Open the door," as emotions began to choke her.

"Open the door," she yelled weeping.

A force from the other side pushed the door open.

"What's wrong, Arte?"

"What in the hell is going on?" yelled Arteah. "Why was the door locked?"

"For some reason, this door gets stuck, the lock jams," revealed Paul.

"Stuck? Isn't this a new home, and why didn't you hear me calling and yelling for you?" Arteah expressed in anger.

"Arte, Arte, calm down, darling. I was in the shower, and I did not hear your beautiful voice. I am so sorry I did not hear you call. I would have come quickly. I forgot to tell you not to close the door. Forgive me, *s'il vous plait*," as he reached for a hug from Arteah.

"I just became paranoid. I mean. I really don't know you. When I was locked up in this room, you can imagine the crazy thoughts wondering through my mind. For all I know, you could be a seductive, suave, murderer," expressed Arteah.

"Come on, my Arte," smiled Paul.

"No, I'm serious," Arteah firmly looked.

"Arte, the way we made love in Tennessee should tell you there is nothing to worry about," said the Frenchman.

"Let's enjoy our evening, Arte," suggested Paul.

"Alright, but let me reapply my lipstick," Arteah said.

She refreshed her face and emotionally pulled herself together. Paul took her to Café Rabelais for fine dining and dancing.

"Did you enjoy your meal?" Paul asked.

"Yes, and this wine has simmered me," revealed Arteah.

"I'm glad you are enjoying yourself. Arte, you must know I would never do anything to harm you ever. I have been searching for a lifetime. Never would I jeopardize your happiness, my Arte."

Thank you. I kind of feel that, but I think it's my own disappointments from the past that have left me a bit edgy," Arteah confessed.

"Arte, I only want to see you smile from the heart. That makes me happy," Paul expressed.

Paul showed Arteah the time of her life with his suave moves on the dance floor. He showed her new swing dance steps. She laughed the night away in her burnt red shimmering gown. The exotic, vivacious American and the suave, romantic Frenchman returned to his haven. He undressed her from the back. She could feel the wind of his breath make her golden skin tingle with erotic sensations. She felt like immediately surrendering, but she knew she had to take the makeup off her face.

"Paul, I need to clean my face."

"Arte, after you do that, will you slip into one of those sexy nightgowns for you, not for me, but for you?"

Arteah could not believe her ears or eyes. Paul worked on her emotionally; she turned into a stream of water, releasing her flow of recent tensions downstream. Upon Paul's request, she cleansed her face and put the long white, satin and lace nightgown on for her. Paul lifted her up and kissed her passionately, placing her in the bed.

"I want you to get a good night's rest; we have a full day tomorrow. I want you to take it all in," Paul whispered.

"What are we doing tomorrow?" asked Arteah, smiling blissfully.

"Surprise. I can't tell you, but I think you probably know."

"Paul, I can't recall my last pleasant surprise."

"Good night, Arte. I am so glad you have journeyed here."

"Good night, Paul."

The sun awoke Paul, but Arteah rested in a deep slumber. Paul did not want to awaken her immediately. He prepared breakfast. He was certain she would not forget a French style breakfast.

"Arte," as he kissed her on the cheek, "Wake up; we have a full adventurous day."

Arteah, with sleepy eyes, smiled at the freshly cooked breakfast. She bit into her croissant and expressed sincere thankfulness to her new lover.

"Delicious, Paul. What are you not good at? In loving, you are beyond measure, and your cooking alone can seduce any woman! Tell me, Paul, what are you not good at," pleaded Arteah.

"Arte, I don't know. I don't really understand American sports, like baseball. It's so boring, and I could never play football. What damaging use of aggression, but I am good at soccer. What about you darling?" Paul asked, looking into her soul.

"Ok…I'll start creative efforts, and I won't follow through. I won't stick with it. So that's why I feel stuck. I want to be adventurous. Well, I am in a sense adventurous, but I haven't been able to make my something personal into something professional. I never get good enough in my something personal."

"Like what, sweetheart," inquired Paul.

"I bought a 35 mm manual camera. I even went to a couple of photography classes and shot a couple of peculiar shots. I guess I didn't know photography was more in depth than I thought. I stopped having an appetite for it, yet I know I have an eye for it. I can feel pictures. I would love to make a calendar, entitled "Happy Times," expressed Arteah.

"Then why don't you?" asked Paul.

"I'm not professional enough."

"Says who? You say you know you have the eye gift. So why aren't you shooting pictures. Let's go to the camera store first and get you the best camera. They have so many new, upgraded cameras. I think you can move beyond the manual 35 mm camera. Besides, Niagara Falls will be all the scenery you need to capture your first "Happy Times" pictures.

Paul and Arteah dressed and drove to the camera store downtown. She picked the top of the line camera that the salesperson recommended, and was given a quick lesson in working it. Paul loved to see the gleam of adventure and satisfaction in Arteah's eyes. Soon after, they set off for the drive to Niagara Falls.

"It's so clean here, and everything is in English and French," noticed Arteah.

"We have two official languages here," explained Paul.

"Neat," responded Arteah.

Arteah snapped shots along the way. As Paul found a parking space, Arteah could see glimpses of the falls. Her excitement began to show.

"We must be here. Niagara Falls!" she chanted.

The young lovers both took in the sights. Paul took pictures of Arteah grinning and laughing, and she took pictures of him posing dignified. They visited the museum and gift shops before taking the tour boat ride under the fall.

"Wow, this has been so much fun. I can't remember the last time I had this much fun," Arteah said.

"I love to see you radiate. I promised you there would be not regrets. Are you pleased you made the trip?" asked Paul.

"I am delighted. It feels like a dream, a fantasy," expressed Arteah.

They ate at a nearby restaurant, before making the drive back to Paul's haven.

Paul poured her a glass of chilled, Moet champagne. As they sat nude in the Jacuzzi together, Paul expressed, "Your beauty is exquisite Arte. You really do drive me crazy. You are sultry, sexy, sophisticated, sassy, and yet simple. I love your nature. Simply, I love it, Arte."

With intensity, his tongue found hers. Her arms and legs opened to receive warmth with thrilling anticipation. The bubbling water provided her external relaxation and his throbbing tool offered her internal joy.

"How do I feel?" tenderly asked Paul.

"Tell me Arte. How do I feel?" Paul asked again, glimpsing into her soul.

"You feel like a strong, dark, wet log traveling deep, deep down my river," replied Arteah.

"Arte, I feel your river only surrenders to the passion of my log. Your river lets me travel wherever. *Merci.*"

At the sound of his voice crescendo, he said, "Arte, I'm traveling, traveling."

Arteah's inner thighs were trembling. Her body released every emotion to freedom.

"Traveling…Traveling."

"Where?" whispered Arteah.

"Your home. Home," as he soon collapsed in tranquility over her body.

Deep breathing was all they could do. As mid-morning had finally awoken the two lovers, they both wondered how they made it to the bedroom.

"Good morning, my Arte," Paul whispered.

"Hi," Arteah replied sluggishly.

"You were especially wonderful last night. You…are breathtaking."

"Thank you, Paul."

Eventually Arteah rolled out of bed into a warm sea salt bath. The two ate Paul's signature French style breakfast. After breakfast, Paul gave Arteah one of his luggage bags to pack all her new items back to Chicago.

"I guess I'll have to check this one in," expressed Arteah.

"My love, you will have help when you get back to Chicago. I don't want you straining anything on your body."

The lovers took a few more pictures of each other.

"I'll put them in the shop, after I leave the airport, and I'll send the pictures to you this week," Arteah informed.

"Let me know how much the development of the pictures are so I can reimburse you."

"Wow, Paul. You really take thoughtfulness to another level," Arteah expressed.

They held hands in the car in route to the Toronto Pearson International Airport. He, at every opportunity, reached over to kiss his long desired lover.

"I'm going to miss you. You have changed my life. I am so happy you visited me," freely expressed Paul.

"Thank you for showing me fun again, and taking my mind and body to another level. More than that, I appreciate you for making me feel most special. Thank you," expressed Arteah.

After checking her luggage, Paul and Arteah kissed and snuggled one last time before she eventually boarded the plane returning to her familiar world in Chicago, Illinois.

Chapter 9

Tennessee defeated Jacksonville 41-6 in the playoffs.

"Most people have doubted this team all year, because we have so many new faces, including a new quarterback. They wondered if Joe Jackson would learn all of the offensive plays in time to start the season. Having him apart of this team marks a new era in the Tennessee organization," addressed the head coach in a televised interview. Midseason, the confidence in winning football games had been restored. A winning attitude had infected the entire team. The head coach was most proud of the team's focus, work ethic, and confidence.

Andre also had plenty to do with the new sense of morale of the team. Every practice and game, he was hyper, intense, and competitive. The wide receiver often chanted, "Our destiny. Baby…We hold the key. Des-ti-ny…We hold the key. Of-fense. Kicks Ass!! De-fense. Kicks Ass!! Of-fense. Kicks Ass!! De-fense. Kicks Ass!! The team anxiously prepared for the game against Chicago.

Andre often thought of his mother, Arteah, and his hometown. He had not heard from Arteah since she left Tennessee. On an evening, during his relaxation time, he telephoned his mother to check in on her and to make plans for his limited visit to Chicago.

"Hi, Mamma," greeted Andre.

"Hey baby. I hadn't heard from you in a while. How's my baby?" asked Mrs. Patterson.

"Good, Mamma. Real good. You know we are coming to Chicago for playoffs this week, and we have to at least have dinner together."

"Sure, baby. Have you talked to little Miss Arteah. Ask her to join us. I'd love to see her too," suggested Mrs. Patterson.

"I'll see what I can do. I'll ask Joe to come with us too," added Andre.

"Ok."

"My agent's office will call you. Love you momma. Can't wait to see you," affirmed Andre.

"Me too. Bye baby," replied his mother.

Andre reflected with a smile knowing how fortunate he was to have the sweetest, caring and supportive mother. He dialed Arteah's number.

"Hey Art. This is 'Dre. I'm calling to see how you are doing," he talked to her voice mail.

"I'll be in Chicago this weekend, and hopefully you can come to dinner with Mom, Joe, and me, if your schedule permits. Art, I'd really love to see you. My agent will call you with the location. Thanks, bye," expressed Andre.

Andre went into the living room where his roommate was watching television.

"What's up, man?" asked Andre.

"Nothing. Just watching old re-runs," Joe replied.

"Hey, this weekend, are your parents going up to the game," Andre inquired.

"I doubt it," stated Joe.

"Is everything alright at home? I don't think I've ever met your parents. Nobody's sick, are they?" Andre curiously prodded.

"No," Joe responded as brief as possible.

"Well, man, my mom and hopefully Arteah are going to meet me for dinner. You're welcome to join us," Andre offered.

"Thanks. I appreciate the offer," accepted Joe.

They talked and made jokes for a while before retiring to their own bedrooms.

Joe felt like he should at least call home to let his parents know the team made it to the playoffs, just in case they did not watch the news.

"Ma? Sorry it's so late. How is everybody? Asked Joe.

"Alright. How are you? You miss the family yet?" asked Mrs. Jackson.

"Of course, I miss ya'll. That's why I was calling to see if everybody wanted to fly up to Chicago this weekend. We've advanced in the playoffs, and I'd love for my family to be there," asked Joe.

"Joe, you know it's too many of us to fly way to Chicago," explained Mrs. Jackson.

"Don't worry about that. I just want you and Pa and the little ones to come to at least one game my rookie year," pleaded Joe.

"There you go again, trying to flash money in our faces. That's your money. We can't afford to just fly to Chicago. It's too expensive. Besides, we have a Sunday evening praise concert at the church," Mrs. Patterson replied, rejecting her eldest son's offer.

"Ma, what is wrong with you. The church will be there if you got away for one Sunday," remarked Joe.

"So when was the last time you've seen the inside of a church," asked his mother.

"Ma, I pray everyday and read the scriptures often. I treat people nicely, and I follow the straight and narrow path," Joe answered.

"Maybe you are fooling yourself to think you are following the righteous path, when you could be sewing bad seeds," preached his mother.

"What are you talking about, sewing bad seed?" Joe intensely asked of his mother.

"Not going to church like you were raised is developing and practicing bad habits. Only God knows what horrible things may be in store for you. I'm going to pray for your safe return home. You are reminding me of the Prodical son, and you know the story of the Prodical son. Ma does not want you to be the Modern version of the good Bible's Prodical son. I love you."

"Ma, I gotta go. Send everybody my love," he said.

His conversation with his mother gave him a headache. He thought, "Why is she talking so absurd? What is this really about? Is something wrong with my religious beliefs? Is there something wrong with me? I can't believe she won't allow me to fly my brothers and sister up to the game!" His thoughts rapidly exhausted him into a deep slumber.

Arteah received the message to meet Andre and his mother for dinner at one of the finest steakhouses downtown. She met the party there, if no more than to be polite.

"Hi, Mrs. Patterson," she said as she hugged Andre's mother.

"Baby, it's so good to see you again. I'm glad you could come," expressed Mrs. Patterson.

"Thank you," said Arteah as she made her way to greet and hug Andre.

"What's up, girl? You couldn't even call a brother when you got back to Chi-Town," he joked as he lifted her up, displaying affection.

"Andre, I've been busy," added Arteah.

"Doing what?"

"None of your business," quipped Arteah.

"Oh, it's like that, huh?" asked Andre.

"Oh, you know I am a teacher, plus I took a little trip to Toronto, Canada," explained Arteah.

"Oh!" smiled Andre.

"Joe, if you don't come here and give me a hug. You act like you don't remember me. I could tell a few jokes, but I won't. I'm going to be very nice to Andre, tonight," Arteah said with a grin.

"How have you been? Arteah, you look great," Joe expressed.

"Boy, you still know how to flatter me," said Arteah.

"Something's different about you. Your hair is very curly. You wear that hairstyle nicely," added Joe.

"You noticed. Joe, you won't believe it; my hairdresser rolled my hair on straws," explained Arteah.

"Baby, what kind of straws," inquired Mrs. Patterson.

"You know, real straws. McDonald Shake straws," she laughed boisterously.

"Wow, that is so creative," said Joe.

"I think the style started in Detroit," Arteah revealed.

"Well, I'm ready for a hot, sizzling, steak, aren't you all?" Andre said, attempting to change the subject.

"Yes," everyone replied agreeably.

They were soon seated. They ordered savoring platters, feasted, and conversed with deep felt sincerity and an abundance of laughter.

Joe immediately noticed what a genuinely supportive mother Andre had. He admired, but secretly envied their relationship. Joe could see the joy in Andre's mom's eyes and how proud she was of her only son.

As Joe glanced and listened to Arteah, he knew more than ever that her internal beauty matched her external beauty. He felt that Andre took Arteah's friendship for granted. Andre could not value and give honor to her worth. Secretly, he wished Arteah were his girlfriend, someone he could talk to and share a sweet intimacy with.

They all ate ice cream for dessert. Soon, thereafter, Arteah informed everyone she had to meet her best friend across town.

"Thanks for inviting me. It's good seeing all of you. Good luck, Andre and Joe in the game. Mrs. Patterson, I know we'll be sitting next to one another. Take care. Bye," Arteah said.

After everyone left, Andre spent time with his mother at her home. Joe rested in his hotel room alone.

Arteah met up with Sherika at the Pepper's Poetry Street Lounge. They caught up with the happenings in each other's lives. Sherika surprised Arteah with her very public poetry debut, entitled "Surviving; Living." Arteah was astonished as she listened to Sherika's deliverance of her poem.

I, for survival, have learned to love myself.

I, for survival, have learned to fill my cup with self love.

I, for survival, have learned to not give away what is precious
to me.

I, for survival, have learned to say no and mean it.

I, for survival, have learned to tread water;

Now,...

I, to live, have learned how to swim.

I, to live, have learned how to savor a moment, every moment,
     No matter how small or grand.

I, to live, have learned that I must surrender to my passion (in
craft).

I, to live, must see the cup as half full.

Simpy...

To live means I've long ago mastered survival, and

Survival is no longer a word I can relate to.

To live means, I possess the highest of faith in my destiny and
path,

My connection with the All Source.

No longer a survivor, but Alive;

Living joyously towards my new state of being.

Applause filled the room. As Sherika took her seat, standing listeners touched her on the shoulder in appreciation.

"Girl, I didn't know you have writing talents, plus delivery skills! When did you start writing?" inquired Arteah.

"Since graduating," Sherika revealed.

"Girl, I felt that poem. Can I get a copy?" asked Arteah.

"Certainly."

"You know I have a new hobby too," expressed Arteah.

"What?"

"Photography. Paul believes I can do this. In fact, I am doing it. I developed the pictures I took in Niagara Falls this morning. They are breathtaking. I really have a natural eye," added Arteah.

"Congrats to new hobbies," Sherika said, raising her drink.

Arteah returned to her cozy apartment. The telephone rang.

"*Mon amour, Arte?* How was your day? Tell me it was beautiful."

"Yes, Paul. It's been beautiful. My best friend surprised me with her new talent. She recited her poem at the poetry lounge. It was entitled "Survival; Living," Wow, was it deep. Plus I had dinner with an old classmate, his mother, and roommate" Arteah shared enthusiastically.

"Great. So you had fun?" inquired Paul.

"Not nearly the amount of fun I had with you at Niagara Falls. Oh yeah, I finally developed the pictures. They are beyond beautiful," expressed Arteah.

"Arte, that's your photography work. I looked into photography classes for you. They begin in January at the Art and Design School there in Chicago. Would you be interested in attending?" Paul asked.

"Yes, absolutely," replied Arteah.

"I'll give you my credit card number, so you can register on-line," Paul offered.

"You don't have to do that. Your thoughtfulness is enough," interjected Arteah.

"I want to give you the gift, because you are so filled with life and beauty. I insist, Arte. *S'il vous plait*," pleaded the Canadian Frenchman.

"Alright. Thank you. Hey, Paul, I really must get sleep tonight," conveyed Arteah.

"So you are not going to let me titillate your mind tonight? Let me make love to you over the phone. You deserve it, Arte," Paul seductively suggested.

"I will fall asleep in the middle of the act," she chuckled.

"I want to sit at the bottom of your waterfall. Your waterfall is more beautiful than the waterfalls in Brazil. Would you shower me?" the Frenchman expressed.

"Oh, my goodness. Now you are driving me crazy."

"That's my intent."

"Tomorrow, make love to me tomorrow, please. I'll need for you to make love to me tomorrow, and in French, but of course with that English translation," she pleaded.

"Ok, my Arte. I'll make love to you tomorrow. Sleep in peace. I treasure and adore you Arte," Paul affirmed.

"Good night, Paul," Arteah replied as she hung up the phone and fell asleep.

Chapter 10

The game began at noon. The brisk, cold air was normal for Chicago football fans. They indulged in the weather. Chicago had scored the first touchdown of the game. The Chicago fans expressed their intense excitement. Arteah bought her new camera to practice her photography as she conversed with Mrs. Patterson about her son.

"Did you have fun when you visited Andre?" asked Mrs. Patterson.

"Yes, Ma'am. It was eventful. I didn't know what to expect," Arteah expressed.

"Good, baby. Good. Andre and you are young people. You should be enjoying yourselves," informed his mother.

"Thank you. I am beginning to enjoy life beyond my wildest expectations," Arteah shared.

"You look good, and I'm glad to see you are taking care of yourself," said Mrs. Patterson.

As they focused in on the game, Tennessee just scored their first touchdown. The Chicago fans booed. It did not take an expert in football to know it was going to be a close game. Andre,

Joe, and the rest of the Sphinx team had been doing their jobs effectively. After the defensive and offensive coaches gave their play plans for the 2nd halt, Andre once again led the team in an uplifting chant.

Our Destiny. Baby..We hold the key.

Des-ti-ny…We hold the key.

Of-fense…Kicks ass! De-fense…Kicks Ass!

Of-fence…Kicks ass! De-fense..Kicks Ass!

The locker room was in an uproar. Onward to the third quarter, where Tennessee was dominant on both sides of the ball. The adrenaline, filled rushes of running back; Myers stabilized a Tennessee 21-14 lead by the end of the third quarter. The Chicago crowd had considerably mellowed in cheers.

In excitement, Arteah expressed, "Mrs. Patterson, I think if Tennessee's defense does their job and no magic happens, this is Tennessee's victory!"

"I believe so," affirmed Mrs. Patterson.

Going into the fourth quarter, the Chicago team grew desperate and scored to tie the game 21-21. Joe became excited, because he knew the coaching staff would disregard their running game and start passing more. With the game tied, the coaching staff quickly gave Joe the no huddle offensive plays. Joe knew he had to score quickly in order to win this game in Chicago. Out of the twelve plays Joe received, ten were passing and two were running plays. This was a quarterback's dream.

As Joe and the team took the field on their own 30-yard line, he knew he had to step up as a leader to ensure his team's victory. Walking into the huddle, he demanded everybody's attention. He called three plays out to the offense that would be run quickly and swiftly. He stopped and turned to Andre and simply gave a wink.

As Tennessee's offensive team lined up, the Chicago defense dug in. Joe took a snap from the center and back peddled five yards. As he looked down field for Andre, he saw that Andre was open. He threw the football to his roommate for a 20-yard gain. The following play was a fired run play that gained 15 yards. With Tennessee heading for the in zone with first in ten, Joe knew it was now or never to score. The Tennessee coaching staff instructed him to call time out in order to discuss the proper play.

In the time out, Joe received a rare passing play from the coaches. The offense lined up as Joe scanned the field, looking for a weakness in Chicago's defense. As he prepared for the snap from the center, he could see the Chicago's defense cheating up into position for a blitz. At that moment, he knew he had to get rid of the ball quickly in order for the play to work. The center hiked the ball. Joe back peddled three steps and saw his teammate going towards the in zone. Jackson stepped up and threw the football with the right, magical touch. He knew this was a touchdown pass.

In a split second, Joe saw Chicago's free safety come over and intercept his touchdown pass. Joe focused in on the safety, as three of his teammates missed tackling the player who intercepted the ball. As he ran towards the approaching safety, he knew he had to position himself right to make the tackle. Hinging at the safety to tackle him, Joe felt the presence of a blocker out of the corner of his right eye. The quarterback then felt a massive blow in his lower back, as he was being knocked to the ground. As the pain intensified in his lower back, he could hear dense background cheers of the Chicago fans, celebrating their touchdown, all because of his costly mistake.

As Joe attempted to leave the field, he could not pick himself up to walk off. Every time he tried to get up, the pain forced him to the ground. At that moment, he knew something was terribly wrong. A crowd of teammates, trainers and coaches soon gathered around him to ask the usual medical questions like "Where does it hurt? Can you move?" Joe looked up towards his teammates and coaches where he recognized voices, but not their blurred faces, because of the pain. Taking deep breaths as instructed by the trainer, he felt more stable at that moment, but at the same time excruciating pain persisted in his lower back. The trainer and coaches helped load Joe on the gurney. He was strapped down for safety precautions to protect his spine.

In Joe's mind, he never imagined he would leave the football field this way. At the same time, he noticed the Chicago stands fell to a dead silence due to his injury on the field. As he was being carted off the field, Andre ran up to his roommate and told him,

"The fans want to hear from you. Give a signal or something that you're OK,"

Joe raised his right hand in the air, and the fans erupted with cheers and applause for him to get better. As the cart went in the dark tunnel, Joe felt himself fall unconscious.

"Oh my gosh Joe is hurt, Mrs. Patterson. I wonder does his family know, since they didn't come to the game," expressed Arteah.

"I'm sure his family is watching the game at home," replied Andre's mother.

The football players resumed on the field to finish the intense fourth quarter. The dynamic game continued into overtime with Tennessee winning with a field goal!

After the game, Mrs. Patterson and Arteah celebrated with Andre.

"Great game, Andre," said Arteah.

"Wasn't it intense? I had so much anxiety when Joe left the game," expressed Andre.

"Where is he? Is he OK?" asked Arteah.

"They rushed him to the hospital. He won't be able to fly back with the team today.

"But is he alright?" asked Mrs. Patterson, showing deep sincerity.

"Momma, we won't know until they run all the tests."

"Since I have to fly back, I'd appreciate if you would call the hospital later and check on him," Andre asked Arteah.

"Do you know which hospital, Andre," questioned Arteah.

"I imagine the closet one to this stadium."

"I'll call the hospitals and see," volunteered Arteah.

"I'd imagine his parents are worried crazy, since they didn't get a chance to come to the game," said Mrs. Patterson.

Andre spent the rest of his time signing autographs, taking pictures, and conversing with his fans, mother and Arteah, until it was time to get on the bus. Eventually, the team was taken to the airport and flown back to Tennessee.

Chapter 11

A rteah made it through the congested parking lot to her car. She listened to her cellular phone messages. Paul had left the most thoughtful message. She immediately called him.

"Hey hon," greeted Arteah.

"How's my Arte," asked Paul.

"Good. I'm leaving the football game," informed Arteah.

"Did you have fun?" Paul inquired.

"Yes, I did, but my buddy's teammate got hurt in the game and was rushed to the hospital."

"So sorry to hear that. I'll never understand that sport. It's so American. So…are you going to visit this guy?" asked Paul.

"Well, I guess I could. I was going to just call the hospital and leave a message for him. I guess it would be more personable to go visit him, especially since his parents didn't get a chance to come to the game, and I didn't see his girlfriend there," expressed Arteah.

"Yes, go Arteah. I'm certain he'd appreciate your support. That's what I adore about you. You are so caring and thoughtful. I miss you Arte. So when am I going to see your lovely smile and your sultry eyes? Tell me when. Don't make me wait so long, Arte," Paul whispered.

"Honey, don't sound so sexy on this phone. You don't want me to have a wreck, do you?"

"Arte, you should just pull over on the highway and let me make love to your mind."

"Tantalize me…tonight," requested Arteah.

"*Mon amour*, why wait? If I were in the car with you, I would let the window down while unfastening your bra. The sensations of the cold breeze would allow your nipples to harden, if I were there in that car with you right now. My tongue would then warm up your nipples and caress them gently until you almost lose control of the car. Every little and big thing I do to you will be in sheer worship of your exotic temple."

"You have me beyond aroused, to say the least. Honey. I really want to continue with this erotic conversation, but I'm approaching the hospital and before I stop, I want to call to make sure he is there," Arteah interjected.

"Alright. I'll go easy on you for now. Let me know if he's ok. I just can't wait to see you soon," said Paul.

"Me too, miss you," expressed Arteah.

Arteah had confirmation Joe was rushed to the Northwestern Memorial Hospital. They had already moved him to Internal Medicine. The doctors were awaiting lab and x-rays results. Joe was hooked up to the IV. Arteah felt deep emotions as she looked into his room, seeing him in such a vulnerable state. His throwing arm was bandaged. Taking a deep breath, she walked in the room and whispered his name.

"Joe. Joe, it's Arteah," she softly spoke.

She immediately realized he was in a deep slumber. Grabbing his hand, she sat with him, offering a silent prayer, "Be healed, Joe." Nearly 20 minutes had passed before Joe eventually awoke in a blurred state. He looked over to see Arteah's golden skin plus he could feel her warm tender hands holding his own. In a deep, slow voice, Joe asked, "Arteah, what are you doing here?"

Arteah, looking into his greenish blue eyes said, "I just came to check in on you. I hope you don't mind."

Joe smiled, "Sure, I don't mind. I'm glad to see a familiar face."

"Did someone notify your parents which hospital you're in so they won't be worried?" inquired Arteah.

"I don't know," replied Joe.

"Do you want me to call them to give a status? They probably are worried," suggested Arteah.

"That's ok. I'll call later," Joe remarked.

"Are you sure? It's no problem."

"Yes, I'm sure. You are all the family I need right now," expressed Joe.

"Thank you. That's sweet."

"No, Arteah. Thank you, for going out of your way to come see me. This means more than you'll ever know. It really touches my heart. You are an amazing, kind hearted woman," Joe revealed.

Joe smiled at her and gazed into her Tootsie-colored brown eyes. This was the first time he could boldly stare at her and admire her beautiful face. As Arteah starred back at him, she wondered why Joe did not have a girlfriend. She thought he was one of the nicest, and most honorable men she had ever met.

However, she knew now was not the time to ask him about his personal life.

"Well, Joe. The team persevered to win. Can you believe Andre said he had a major anxiety attack when you came out of the game?" Arteah tried to make light humor of the situation.

"Anxiety attack? That doesn't sound like Andre," Joe chuckled.

"Really. He said he had a major anxiety attack, worrying about his roommate and the rest of the game."

The doctor knocked on the door, and came in.

"Joe, I see your pretty, gorgeous girlfriend is here. Hello, I'm Dr. Schuberg."

"Nice to meet you," greeted Arteah with a smile.

"Doc, Arteah is a friend," confessed Joe."

"How can you keep someone as beautiful as her simply as your friend," the doctor flirted jokingly.

"Thanks Doc," said Arteah.

Joe and Arteah looked at one another and smiled.

"You two, I'll cut through the chase. You have a kidney bruised that's going to take some time to heal, and of course, you have a dislocated shoulder that should not take too long. You're going to have to be out for the rest of the season to take precautionary measures," informed Dr. Schuberg.

"Doc, we only have about two or three games left, depending how far we go in the playoffs."

"I understand all of that, but if you want longevity in the league, you are going to have to set out for a couple of games. Other than that, right now, I'm going to prescribe something for your pain. Is there anything you'd like to ask me?" inquired Dr. Schuberg.

"No, I don't have any question. I just have to adjust somehow," Joe expressed.

"Oh, I do understand. Look on the bright side. Miss, if you take care of this guy, I'm certain he'll have a smooth recovery. We'll check him out in the morning."

"I'll do my best," Arteah said.

"Thank you Doc," said Joe as the doctor was leaving.

Joe's face looked disappointed. The season was over for him, plus he had injuries he had never sustained before.

"Well, Joe. That's good news. You can fly back to Tennessee tomorrow and rest in your own bed," said Arteah.

"Yeah, you're right. You are so positive," Joe noticed. "Arteah, you don't have to stick around here. I'm sure you have a busy schedule. Thank you so much for going out of your way to check on me. I truly appreciate it," reiterated Joe.

"No problem. How are you getting to the airport tomorrow?"

The organization has someone to take me, to make sure I get back to Tennessee safely.

The two acquaintances talked a brief time longer before Arteah later left the hospital.

Chapter 12

Back in Tennessee, Andre had settled in by 9 pm. His agent had left a message to meet him for a nightcap. He was considering canceling, because he was exhausted from the game and travel. His phone rang before he could make the call.

"Andre, Fantastic game!! I'm waiting on you at the Grill. I have good news for you. Come on down," said his agent.

"Man, I am exhausted."

"Not you Andre, Mr. Everlast. How could you be exhausted after winning the game in Chicago?" his agent hyped.

"Alright. Alright! I'll be there," affirmed Andre.

Andre drove to see his agent.

"Good to see you," greeted his agent with a handshake hug.

"You too. So what's the good news that couldn't wait?" inquired Andre.

"The deal went through," his agent expressed.

"Which deal?"

"The clothing deal with C-style. They want to use you to promote their sporting/casual line. The contract is worth $15 million for three years," explained his agent.

"What? For real?" Andre questioned exctitingly.

"This occasion calls for a real celebration," commented his agent.

The waitress took their drink orders.

"You know man. I am living the good life. It's a shame most people live in scarcity and I, and a few others, are fortunate to live in so much excess. Luck is a motherfucker, ain't it? Damn, I got it going on!"

"I knew I could leave it to you to toot your own horn," his agent joked.

"Thanks for capturing this deal for me," Andre said, showing a sense of gratitude.

"Cheers," said his agent.

"Here's to the good, lavish life," Andre boisterously toasted.

A few fans came over to the table, but Andre could not help but notice this classy woman setting in the booth alone. The brunette had striking features that immediately caught his eye. The woman did not gaze over towards him. Andre kept starring. She was reading a novel, while sipping on hot chocolate with whip cream. Andre had a curiosity to meet this self entertained woman.

Usually at this point in a social outing, all women would have taken notice of him or given him the temptress eye, but she had not. It was something mystical about the brunette woman's presence. Andre was intrigued. So he went to make acquaintance.

"Hi. I'm Andre. What's your name?"

"Why?"

"I noticed you are a beautiful woman out tonight alone," the celebrating athlete said.

"Actually, I'm working."

"I see you are deep into that book. Is it interesting like you?" he charmed.

"Depends on your interest," she quipped.

"So can I know your name, beautiful," asked Andre.

"Sure. I'm Shabella," she greeted, extending her hand.

"Sha-bel-la," he said smoothly.

"Even your name is interesting."

"Thanks."

"Can I buy you a drink?"

No, that won't be necessary…Andre? Right? I am about to leave in a moment," Shabella said.

Andre took her hand and kissed it, and simply asked, "Can I spend the rest of the evening with you?"

"There is a price; I must warn you."

"Beautiful, I can see you are priceless. Do you feel comfortable coming to my place or back to yours?" he asked.

"My place is probably more suitable," she informed.

"Cool. Let me pay my tab, say goodbye to a friend, and then I'll be ready to go," Andre said.

"I'll meet you outside," Shabella confirmed.

Andre paid his tab and said farewell to his agent. He felt he deserved to be entertained by the striking woman, since he had entertained millions of fans earlier. He followed her to her condo. He got out of his car and rushed to open her car door for her.

"What a serving man," she commented.

"My pleasure, Miss Sha-bel-la," Andre eloquently said.

The celebrating athlete knew he was in store for an interesting, mind-blowing night.

"Would you like a glass of wine?" asked the sultry woman.

"No thanks. Just iced water," he replied. "I have to train in the morning, and I don't want to be too sluggish."

"Oh, so I assume you are an athlete," inquired Miss Shabella.

"Yes," affirmed Andre. He thought she already knew, especially considering the team made it to the playoffs. He rationalized that she must live in seclusion with her head always in a book.

"I see you love to read," he commented about seeing her overflowing bookcases.

"Reading and collecting great books is one of my hobbies," she conversed.

"Interesting," Joe said as he moved in closer to her to kiss her lips.

"Gosh, you are pretty, Sha-bel-la," he whispered in her ear.

She looked at him feeling every moment of sensations. She gazed into his eyes, before he lifted her skirt up in the moment of passion. Andre squeezed her round butt and stroked his strong hands up her neck to the back of her head. He was so attracted to the mysterious woman with the unknown last name. Few words were exchanged, just moans of sensations. Andre focused on satisfying her physically with no words, just actions. As the two acquaintances laid in Shabella's bed completely satisfied and exhausted, Shabella almost forget she was working. The passionate act of sex felt too close to making love that she did not know what to do.

"Damn, he's good in bed," she thought. "Babygirl, be professional about this. Be professional."

At 3 a.m., she awoke Andre and said," You're staying over the limit time."

"What? Come here and let me put my arms around you, Sha…Sha..bella," Andre whispered.

"No, listen buddy. You are over the limit, which means you owe me $5,000 for my services."

"What are you talking about?" asked Andre as he began to open his eyes.

"Don't play crazy. I told you I was working, and it would cost you a fee."

"So, what are you saying? You are a prostitute?"

"Boy, don't play crazy like you didn't know I am a high class prostitute. I work that restaurant all the time."

"What? I didn't know," explained Andre.

"Bullshit. Because I told you it would cost you. So give me my $5,000 now, so I can fully relax in my home without you laying in my bed," Shabella firmly said.

"Look, I don't carry $5,000 around. I don't have it."

"Bullshit. I know you are a star athlete. I'm not that naïve," she said.

"Look, I don't have to pay for nothing, especially sex," Andre remarked. With haste, he got out of the bed naked to put his briefs on.

"Hold up one moment, buster. Don't even make this a nasty situation, where I have to be in charge of collections, too."

"Look Shabella. I gotta go. Nice meeting you, but you might wanna go get some psychological help, if you really expect me to believe you are a prostitute," Andre said.

Shabella snapped.

"Let's see how much psychological help you are going to need when I shoot your ass," she forcefully said, pulling her handgun from under her bed. She aimed the gun at Andre and yelled, "Nigga, pay me my money, all $5,000 of it. See, I ain't going to kill you. Tell me Andre, Mr. Athlete, how much psychological help would you need, if I were to shoot you right in the right knee. Pow. How much Prozac would you need to recover when your career would be cut mighty short? So pay me my motherfucking money, now!"

"Girl, don't make me want to call you out of your name," Andre warned.

"Oh, you wanna call me a bitch. See, Nigga. You are the dog, just laying around. You don't know a damn thing about me, not one damned thing, but you think I'm a bitch. Actually I'm a ho, because bitches just get laid, but ho's get paid. You are really pissing me off right now," as verbal rage poured from her mouth.

At that moment, Andre realized he had to be a bit more selective about his chosen words. Anything could make her snap. Shabella was a pretty bomb, calculated to explode.

"No I don't think you are a bitch," Andre said calmly.

"I know what you're thinking. It's all in your actions. See, buster, I've seen a lot of you athletes come and go. How old do you think I am?"

"I don't know. 25?" he answered.

She laughed, "Nigga, I'm 48. I know I look good. I'm in the business to look good. Just like you have to stay fit, I stay fit to keep my contracts coming too, Nigga. Believe me, I'll be around after you're gone. I can't begin to name the star atletes who have afforded me my vacations in the South of France and my stock plans. I don't have to worry about a Goddamned thing. I enjoy my job, just like you enjoy your job. It can get intense sometimes like football. I've outlasted O.J's career. Ya'll young niggas think you can just treat a woman any kind of way. Fuck-em and leave them with a heartache. Since it seems to me that you are new at soliciting fucking services, I'll give you a discount. I want $2,000" she demanded.

"I really do not have that kind of money on me," Andre said.

"Cheap Niglet, how much you've got?" she forcefully asked.

"Close to a thousand."

"I don't believe this shit!" She shot off her gun in his direction. The bullet hit the wall. Andre jumped and ran into the living room, trying to escape a living nightmare. She shot again, hitting the bedroom door.

"Give me what you got right now!"

Andre dived to the floor, near the sofa to protect himself.

"Give it to me," shouted the woman in rage.

Trembling, Andre handed over all the cash in his wallet.

"Here, this is all I have on me."

She picked it up and said," Now, Niglet. Get the fuck out!! I ain't gonna tell you no more to get the fuck out of my home. The next shot, I will end your career. Do you still want it in your knee? POW! I love knees, such a vulnerable spot on a player's body."

As she aimed at him, Andre grabbed his keys and crawled to the door, then got up. As he ran out, he was too fearful to call her what he was thinking; Shebella was in his mind a crazy bitch. Sweating and breathing deeply, he ran for his life.

Chapter 13

Arteah called her new lover, Paul, and informed him of Andre's roommate's health status.

"Joe's going to be alright, but he has to sit the rest of the season out," said Arteah.

"I'm disappointed to hear that. I'm certain that has to be mentally torturous to be a professional athlete," Paul said.

"He seems spiritually sound, but I was surprised his parents nor anyone else called while I was in his room to check up on him. That was a little weird, considering his popularity," Arteah conveyed.

"Who knows, Arte. Sometimes you never really know about people and their so-called families," alerted Paul.

"I guess you're right," she responded.

"So how's my Arte? How are you? I'm concerned about you. I wish I were there to rub you down with hot oil," Paul said.

"That would be so nice, Paul,"

"I have to take care of you. You deserve tender care. I need to see you," confessed Paul.

"Paul, I feel your sincerity, but I don't want us to move too fast. It's already been a whirlwind. You've taken me faster than I've ever been before," Arteah revealed.

"I'm not accustomed to this. I know I like you; we click. You treat me so well, simply the best, but I do have fears," Arteah added.

"Don't worry, Arte. We'll take it slower. What if we write one another, call, and then in a month or so, we'll plan to go on another date. Arte, I told you that I am crazy about you, and that's not going to change. You probably have doubts about me making love to you on the first night still. I am not judging you, but I am loving you. I hope you continue to let me. Arte, you are wonderful. You do blow my mind. I will prove to you that I'm crazy about you."

"Thanks, Paul. You have amazed me since the moment I met you in Tennessee. I love the way you make me feel. I feel so beautiful and sexy," expressed Arteah.

"Like I've told you before, you are beautiful, sexy, alluring, smart, humorous, sensational, and more than anything, sweet! And I don't have a problem validating you over and over until it marinates your heart. Any man who gets to have a ten minute conversation with you would instantly fall in love with you like I know I have," Paul genuinely whispered to Arteah. The dark Frenchman seduced her mind with fantasy pleasures.

"You are incredible; however; you make it so challenging courting you slowly. No wonder, I've enjoyed surrendering to you," Arteah expressed in amazement.

"Arte, get some rest. I'm sure it's been a long day for you. My Arte, in time your doubts will disappear. Good night," assured Paul.

"Good night, Paul."

Joe safely returned to Nashville. Facing the reality of his injuries, his spirits felt sluggish. He had been so blessed to not get hurt. He never had any injuries in high school and no serious injuries in college. His religious beliefs made him contemplate why this injury had happened to him. "Could it be like Ma said that 'Working on the Sabbath won't lead to a prosperous life?' Maybe I am not keeping good values," he contemplated.

He checked his voice mail. There were no messages for him. He could not believe no one from his family had called to see if he was all right. The reality of his loneliness deeply set in. This should be the happiest, blessed time in his life, yet the evolved reality was loneliness and a painful injury. Joe grew tired; his faith in goodness suddenly diminished. He called home hoping to be encouraged by his mother, the woman who had loved him from birth.

"Hello, Ma," sluggishly greeted Joe.

"What time is it? Oh heavens. It's late. Joe, how are you? When are you coming home?" immediately asked his mother.

"Did ya'll see the game, Sunday," asked Joe.

"Naw, we've been so busy. You do understand?" asked Mrs. Jackson.

"You know, Ma, I do understand that you're too busy to even notice that I've been in the hospital," exploded Joe.

"What are you talking about?" asked his mother, being caught by surprise.

"I took a bad hit Sunday and had to be rushed to the hospital from the stadium, and nobody from my family seemed to have noticed," Joe expressed in furry.

"Are you ok?"

"Yes, I will be fine, now. I'm out for the season, but Ma, I'm dandy," sarcastically expressed the injured athlete.

"So you'll be able to come home, now, right?"

"That's all you've been concerned about since I've been in Tennessee is when I'm coming home, never concerned about my transition in the league, my transition to a new city. You know I have a one-person household that I have to tend to. I guess you think your household is the only one that matters."

"Joe, we miss you dearly," interjected his mother.

"But will you sacrifice to come see me at my expense? No! You give me some holier than thou excuse. The excuses are so noble, Ma. So noble! I don't want to tell you what I really think of your excuses on why you won't send my baby brothers and sisters up to see me. But I will make sacrifices to come home as soon as I can, so I can do my big brotherly role, to help raise all of them," Joe intensely expressed.

"Don't talk to me like this," said Mrs. Jackson.

"I have to go tend to my ailing body and take my pain killers now. I'll let you know when I'm coming home." "Joe, we love you and miss you," said his mother.

"Sometimes, it's hard to tell. Gotta go," he said, immediately hanging up the phone.

Joe held his head in disbelief. His perfect world was falling apart. Everything that was certain in his life, the love and support of his family and the consistency of his athleticism, was beginning to crumble before his eyes. He could talk to his roommate, Andre, but there was not a high level of intimacy and sincerity in their conversations. He took his medicine and went to bed. As he rested his eyes, he felt a desire to see a picture of Arteah.

He slowly arose out of bed and went in his roommate's room to find a particular photo album. The album was stacked on Andre's lower bookcase shelf. He opened it, briefly staring at the high school photo of Arteah, before taking the picture. He knew Andre would probably not notice it was missing. Joe returned to his bedroom, holding the picture in relief of renewed hope. He knew someone sincerely cared; someone was thoughtful. Arteah was the one person who made him feel appreciated. The image of her in the picture and the remembrance of the intimate moments in the hospital made him not feel so extremely lonely. Her spirit offered him hope, that he could make it through his unforeseen challenges. He drifted into a pleasant dream.

For the next couple of days, Joe and Andre saw very little of each other, because Andre was in practice with the rest of the team for the upcoming game. Andre had not discussed his bizarre night with the prostitute to anyone. He was beyond embarrassed. Andre had been in deep reflection since his life had been put in such danger, but he knew how to focus and channel in to what mattered most, his performance on the field.

That Friday, Joe was home when a Fed Ex package came to the house. He signed for it. It was addressed to Andre Patterson and Joe Jackson, the roommates. He opened the package and noticed that there were two separate envelopes, one with his name and the other with Andre's. He immediately opened his envelope to find a "Get Well" card and some pictures of him in the game. Arteah wrote, "I hope you are making a speedy recovery. Wishing you good health, happiness, and love. Arteah McMorris."

Joe was deeply moved by the card and her kindness, but he noticed she did not leave a return address or telephone number.

Joe looked at Andre's envelope and became instantly tempted to open his. He felt the presence of more pictures in Andre's envelope. His contemplation to open his roommate's envelope was decided when he rationalized that he could easily seal it back. Joe opened the other envelope to find a letter that read, " As promised, here are the pictures, plus a couple of shots of me from Niagara Fall. Wow, was it a Blast! Best wishes in your upcoming game. Holler!! Home skillet. Sincerely, Art." Joe glimpsed at all the pictures. He again fell in rapture with her beauty. She had sent over twenty pictures. Joe picked out the best ones of Arteah and sealed Andre's envelope back.

Joe returned to his bedroom to tape all of the pictures of Arteah up in his closet, a place where his roommate would never check. He moved some clothes around to highlight his new pictures. When he finished decorating, it looked like a small shrine. Starring at her photographed, image reflections, he spoke," *Hey, Arteah,… You are too sweet for just any man. I know and feel a warm connection between us. The way you looked at me at the hospital. I've never have felt that type of affection, ever in my life. I need that, and I will have you. I need you like water. I am so thirsty for you, sugar pie. I think it is time that I say what I need to you. I'm sure you are thinking this too. Why would you go out of your way to tend to me, better than my own family? With you in my life, it would be easy to leave this football roller coaster I've been on since Junior High. I am a screaming eagle. It's time. I know you are looking for a man to come to you with the most sincere intent. You are not the type of woman to chase. So, I will let it be known. It is no doubt in my mind; you will be with me for our lifetimes. Andre has everything, a magical career, the best mother, and you as his friend. All I crave is your warmth and love. That's all that matters.*

The heck with the rest of this world. First, I'll tell Andre my desire and longing to hold you. I'll send for you, and tell you my inner thoughts of my love and affection for you. Then, we'll embrace with a spiritual, passionate kiss."

Joe closed his shrine closet. Thereafter, he fell into a deep slumber.

Chapter 14

The Sunday game quickly arrived. Tennessee faced an embarrassing loss to Baltimore 28-7. Their season was over. The entire team was deeply disappointed and frustrated that they blew their chances for Super Bowl contentions. The next evening, Andre returned home.

Joe said, "Man, I need to talk to you."

"Not now. Shit, man. I have been having these nightmares from hell. Can it wait?" suggested Andre.

"No, not really."

"Man, I just need to crash. I'm sorry. We'll talk later. We got all of the time in the world. Season is over. I can't begin to tell you about these recurring nightmares. Man, I'm just exhausted. I'm beat."

A deep sleep fell over Andre. He slept for over 16 hours straight. When Andre awoke, he reached out to call Arteah.

"I need to see you desperately," requested Andre.

""What's wrong with you?" You sound so sincere," she laughed. "Is your mom ok?"

"Yes, she's fine."

"Why don't you come to Chicago?" Arteah suggested.

"If you come back to Tennessee, I promise to take you to the caves in Chattanooga. I need to see and talk to you, and I don't want to do it over the phone."

"Andre, I have a lot going on now."

"Art, I have to see you. Please, I have something I must tell you in person. I will take care of your hotel arrangements and everything else?" begged Andre.

"Ok, but may I bring my best friend," Arteah bargained.

"Who?"

"Sherika."

"Ok, I'll take care of the arrangements," Andre said ending the conversation.

He jumped out of bed with a semi-restored spirit, and went into the living room to immediately tell Joe about Arteah, returning to Tennessee to visit the caves.

"Hey, she's going to bring her best friend so we can all hang out, if you want to," suggested Andre.

"What?" Joe asked.

Andre's conversation was totally confusing to him. He was clueless why Arteah would bring a female friend for him to meet. Joe assumed she just needed her girlfriend to go shopping with and someone to go get a pedicure with. Thus Joe delayed telling his roommate of his growing warmth and affection for the woman of his dreams.

Andre attempted to explain more about the details of her visit.

"Andre, it sounds like fun. I can't wait to see Arteah again. She was so sweet and considerate to visit me in the hospital. Plus, I'd love to meet her friend," Joe said, confirmed the outing.

Arteah and Sherika flew in the following weekend and had hotel reservations at the same five-star hotel. While Sherika was taking her shower, Andre and Arteah walked downstairs to the Greenhouse Café. Memories of Paul's presences came to Arteah's mind. She smiled. Andre revealed, "Art, I can't wait any longer to tell you. I must tell you now. I need you in my life, and I love you dearly. I am ready to give it a chance in a committed relationship. I'm ready to not just try; I want to do. I want to be there for you. I want to give you my best. You always have deserved it. Now, I'm ready to give you my best. Will you take what I'm offering? We can take it slow. We'll date in Chicago and Tennessee. Hell, we'll date in Paris, until I prove my level of commitment to you. Will you accept this necklace to mark my new level of affection and commitment towards you? I just want to honor you to the highest degree. Will you be my lady, not my main lady, but my only lady, Art?" asked Andre.

"Andre, I am dating someone now."

"But are you committed to him, Art?"

"No, not yet," revealed Arteah.

"Good, I have a chance. Keep this token, this necklace, and grant me a chance. I want to prove to you that I can be focused only on you," begged Andre.

"I don't know. You've got major competition now. Not only is he focused on me, he romances me in unimaginable ways," Arteah confessed.

"That's alright. I love competition. I'll prevail to capture your heart."

"Ok, I'll give you dating time. I can't promise anything more. Just dating time."

"That's all I need. I want to spend the rest of my days making up for my foolishness and selfishness. What's a little competition?"

Andre hugged Arteah and gave her a big kiss on her glossy lips.

Returning to Arteah's room, Andre immediately broke the news to Sherika.

"Sherika, your girl, my home skillet, is going to give me the opportunity to sweep her off her feet. I am crazy about her. I've always admired and adored her, but sewing my oats got the best of me. I'm just glad I realized it before it was too late."

"Really?" said Sherika, checking her best friend's response.

"Yeah, I'm going to give him dating time. That's about it," Arteah clarified.

"Sherika, I can see it in your eyes. I already know she is seeing someone else. I already know. She ain't playing me. I will be her finest suitor. Eventually, she'll have to tell this other guy, bye-boo," Andre said confidently.

"Congrats. As long as you know what you're doing, girl," Sherika said, while noticing the diamond necklace.

After Arteah changed her clothes, they went to the house to pick up Joe, and to tell him the news. Joe, in a state of shock tried to look happy. He had no idea Andre was giving up all his women for Arteah.

"I almost forgot. What did you want to tell me? You keep forgetting," reminded Andre.

"I worship Art too. Doesn't every man?" Joe finally confessed.

"I know. I am so lucking she is giving me, with all of my retired ways, the time of day, especially after all the stuff I've done. Damn, I'm lucky. Just living the good life."

"Congratulation," Joe said.

Andre, Joe, Sherika and Arteah went to the movies. Andre sat near Arteah, who sat next to her friend, Sherika. Joe was silent most of the time. They returned to the house to play games, during which Sherika had a craving for some ice cream. Sherika convinced Andre to drive her to the nearest ice cream parlor.

"Hurry back," Arteah said.

"Girl, why don't you ride with us?" insisted Sherika. "Joe, you too."

"I need to make a couple of urgent phone calls to my parents, anyway," Joe responded.

"I just don't feel like going back out in the cold again until we get ready to go back to the hotel, but you can bring me some German Chocalate, two scoops, please. Thanks," Arteah said.

Arteah was sitting on the sofa, flipping through the cable station, being entertained. After making his call in his bedroom to his family, Joe came into the living room in rage, "How could you do this to us? We had the perfect future, and you choose to share it with Andre. Yeah, you two have history, but do you know how many women have slept in that bed of his? Do you know?" Joe, feeling heightened frustrations, grabbed her and forced her into his bedroom.

He opened the door of his closet. It had been painted Royalty purple and shining gold with pictures of her everywhere.

"Do you know how I've worshipped you with my own shrine to honor you?"

He snapped, "You lied to me and said you two were just old acquaintances reacquainting...I've built my fantasies around you. Now, I have nothing."

"Joe, what has gotten into you?"

"Do you hear me? I have nothing to live for! Not a secure career. Not a family that gives a crap, and now not even you! You know, I'm tired and just sick of being unappreciated, while people like Andre, who have no morals whatsoever come up with golden prizes. They get the major endorsement deals, and sail through life with no injuries, and now to add the cherry atop his cake, he gets the best prize of all, you. What have I done wrong? I pray. I'm religious. I give to the church, and all I really asked for was you, a God-fearing woman with a heart of gold. Arteah, Can't you see, I have nothing, absolutely nothing to live for!"

"Yes, you do Joe. The doctors said you would make a speedy recovery. I know you probably have a lot of anguish and pain from the injury."

"Do you know how much pain it is to just sit around, when nobody cares if you are dead or alive?"

"Joe, you have fans that adore you and look up to you," Arteah said.

"That's all they are; fans! Look. Look!! You are the one thing I desired."

He smashed her head into the pictures. Arteah could not believe what was happening to her.

"Joe, you are hurting me." she cried.

"I'm hurting you; I've never hurt anybody in my entire life."

He cuddled her into his arms and rubbed her head tenderly. Arteah still could not believe what was happening to her. She was a long way from her Canadian excursion. She went into a state of shock as she looked all around the closet, viewing the mélange of pictures of her, including her high school pictures.

She started screaming.

"Be quiet, I'm not going to hurt you. I would never hurt you."

"Let me out of here. I don't know what has gotten into you! Joe, are you having a bad mental reaction to the medication you are taking?"

Joe reached for his handgun on the top shelf.

"Take my life. Kill me. You already have. Do it. Damn it. Do it," he yelled at her with heightened force.

She started screaming louder.

"I can't do that. You got to get it together, Joe. You got to pull it together. I'll help you," Arteah shaking in fear.

"Kill me. Now!! I can't take all of these ranting thoughts ranging through my mind. I haven't had a peaceful sleep in months. Kill me!"

Choking on her words, she sobbed, "I can't kill you."

Grabbing her by her hair, he turned the gun on her to kill her, because she would not meet his demands. Arteah kicked him with her left leg, and attempted to escape at least to the living room. She tried to quickly think, when all she wanted to do was run and scream more for her young life. Yet, she felt his spirit and body haunting her. Coming out of his bedroom, he pointed the gun at her as he got closer and closer upon her, threatening her peaceful life. Although her mind was racing a million miles an hour, she knew she had to stay calm to buy time to think clearly.

"Joe, I really did not know you cared for me. I had no idea. I wished you had just told me. Then so many emotions would not have escalated. And now you want me to end your life?"

"You still don't get it. It's everything!! Everything has collapsed," he said.

"We are young and vital. We have everything to live for," Arteah pleaded.

"I don't. That has never been my sunny outlook. I'm tired of figuring and reconfiguring…and for what! I'm tired of hoping, investing emotions into things and society and people, including my backwards thinking family who don't give a damn," Joe yelled.

"I'm sure your mom and dad love and support you. You would not have gotten so far without them," interjected Arteah.

"Just shut up! You don't know what you are talking about. Don't ever talk about them!! They are not worth talking about! You are making me angry with your psychoanalysis bullshit," Joe snapped in force holding the gun to her forehead.

It was clear Joe was emotionally disturbed.

"Please, Joe! Take the gun away from my head. You are frightening me! Please, I thought we were simply having a conversation!!"

"I'm tired of it all. And you, my last hope, have been the last disappointment I can bear," Joe expressed intensely.

As he aimed the gun in her face, her entire life went in slow motion. Questions surfaced in her mind. *How did I get myself in this position? What do I do? What do I do?* As she starred down the barrel of the gun, she could see a blank stare on his face. Suddenly a tear started to form in his eye, and then rolled down his cheek. A strange half smile formed around his mouth and he said, "It is time for me to go, babygirl." He slowly pointed the gun at his own temple. She knew he was going to do it.

"No! No!! God, no," she screamed as she reached and grabbed the gun. The sound of the discharge was deafening. The heat of the gun burned her hand. As Joe fell to the ground, she was holding the gun so tightly that she fell on top of him. Blood was splattered on her hands and arms. All she could do was scream, scream, and scream!!!

Her body went into convulsions as Arteah cried and yelled for help. She lost all sense of time and surroundings. She was mentally frozen. Suddenly she felt a hand around her waist, pulling her to her feet, pulling her close. It was Andre. As her senses slowly returned, she heard Sherika sobbing in disbelief in the background.

"Oh, my God, I can't believe this. There is blood everywhere," frantically screamed Sherika.

Andre held Arteah to his chest. She looked empty, without emotions.

"Call the ambulance! Call the ambulance and police! Call 911," Andre yelled to Sherika.

As he held Arteah intensely, he stared over Joe's body realizing that the 357 Caliber round had blown away half his head. After what seemed like hours, the city police finally arrived.

Arteah McMorris, 22, was handcuffed and booked for the shooting and killing of Joe Jackson. She talked to the D.A. for hours. Eventually, she was released. As they left the station, Andre hugged Arteah tightly. No words were spoken as they both were too drained to calculate the signs of why.